W9-CFH-478

"Don't touch me! I hate you, Pasqual."

Rhiannon pushed her palms against his chest in desperation. His eyes glinted with amusement. "Hate is the reverse side of the coin to love. I think that it's still love you feel."

"No!" she said wildly, her green eyes flashing. "I'll never love you again!"

"Does that mean I shall be forced to keep you a prisoner forever?" He looked as though the idea appealed to him.

"Kidnapping is a punishable offence," cried Rhiannon, but it was too late. He had already covered her lips with his and the deliberate assault made desire run through her like quicksilver. Her fingers entwined in his hair, wanting to pull him closer. This was how it had been in the beginning... before he had deceived her. How could she let this happen again? Was there no means of escape?

MARGARET MAYO began writing quite by chance when the engineering company she worked for wasn't very busy and she found herself with time on her hands. Today, with more than thirty romance novels to her credit, she admits that writing governs her life to a large extent. When she and her husband holiday—Cornwall is their favorite spot—Margaret always has a notebook and camera on hand and is constantly looking for fresh ideas. She lives in the countryside near Stafford, England.

Books by MARGARET MAYO

HARLEQUIN PRESENTS
963—PASSIONATE VENGEANCE

HARLEQUIN ROMANCE
2086—RAINBOW MAGIC
2118—SEA GYPSY
2280—AFRAID TO LOVE
2327—STORMY AFFAIR
2360—VALLEY OF THE HAWK
2385—BURNING DESIRE
2439—A TASTE OF PARADISE
2474—DIVIDED LOYALTIES
2557—DANGEROUS JOURNEY
2602—RETURN A STRANGER
2795—IMPULSIVE CHALLENGE
2805—AT DAGGERS DRAWN

Don't miss any of our special offers. Write to us at the following address for information on our newest releases.

Harlequin Reader Service
901 Fuhrmann Blvd., P.O. Box 1397, Buffalo, NY 14240
Canadian address: P.O. Box 603,
Fort Erie, Ont. L2A 5X3

MARGARET MAYO

savage affair

Harlequin Books

TORONTO • NEW YORK • LONDON
AMSTERDAM • PARIS • SYDNEY • HAMBURG
STOCKHOLM • ATHENS • TOKYO • MILAN

Harlequin Presents first edition January 1988
ISBN 0-373-11045-6

Original hardcover edition published in 1987
by Mills & Boon Limited

Copyright © 1987 by Margaret Mayo. All rights reserved.
Philippine copyright 1987. Australian copyright 1987.
Cover illustration copyright © 1987 by Wes Lowe.
Except for use in any review, the reproduction or utilization of
this work in whole or in part in any form by any electronic,
mechanical or other means, now known or hereafter invented,
including xerography, photocopying and recording, or in any
information storage or retrieval system, is forbidden without
the permission of the publisher, Harlequin Enterprises Limited,
225 Duncan Mill Road, Don Mills, Ontario, Canada M3B 3K9.

All the characters in this book have no existence outside the
imagination of the author and have no relation whatsoever to
anyone bearing the same name or names. They are not even
distantly inspired by any individual known or unknown to the
author, and all incidents are pure invention.

The Harlequin trademarks, consisting of the words
HARLEQUIN PRESENTS and the portrayal of a Harlequin,
are trademarks of Harlequin Enterprises Limited and are
registered in the Canada Trade Marks Office; the portrayal
of a Harlequin is registered in the United States Patent
and Trademarks Office.

Printed in U.S.A.

CHAPTER ONE

THE LIGHT was fading fast, making it difficult to see clearly, but Rhiannon never took her eyes off the unknown man. He had to be a man. No woman could carve her way through the water quite so fiercely and determinedly.

She sat with her back against a rock, confident that by the time he came out darkness would render her invisible. She was so used to having the beach to herself at this time of day that finding someone here was intriguing.

At length he rose from the water, his shape silhouetted against sky now almost as dark as the sea. He was tall, with wide shoulders and narrow hips, and as he turned to look across the bay she observed a flat taut stomach and muscular chest. There was an arrogant lift to his chin, he had a high noble forehead, and the sinking sun cast a bronze sheen over his statue-like body.

When he headed directly towards her Rhiannon froze. Had he seen her after all? She held her breath, wishing she had made her presence known instead of sitting here like a Peeping Tom, mentally crossing her fingers that he would walk straight past.

She closed her eyes, as if by so doing she could banish him, then gave an involuntary cry as he stumbled over her outstretched leg.

'What the devil?' His Spanish voice was loud and angry and she glanced up to see his powerful body towering over her. Before she could speak one firm hand grabbed her shirt and hauled her to her feet. She felt like a fish dangling from an angler's hook.

'Put me down!' she yelled, answering in his own language, kicking and punching, but not seeming to hurt him. He was strong, very strong, and almost a foot taller than she. She could see a gleam in his eyes and a ruthless thrust to his jaw.

In response to her plea he let go her shirt, but his hands fell instead to her shoulders. And then as his eyes raked her face she felt the tenseness go out of him. He smiled and his teeth gleamed white in the darkness.

'I'm sorry if I startled you,' she said quickly. 'I was watching you swim and——'

'It was suddenly too late to make your presence known?' he finished for her. 'I can understand that.'

His low throaty tone sent a shiver crawling down her spine. It had a sensual sound to it, and despite the fact that she could not properly see him, that she did not know who he was or anything about him, she felt an instant and unwarranted physical awareness.

'I'm glad you're not angry.' Her eyes were wide as she looked up at him, and she tried to ignore the sudden racing of her heart. 'I was afraid you'd think I was prying.'

His fingers began slow circling movements over her shoulderblades. 'I was curious, perhaps, but nothing so sordid as that.' And he moved lower, and lower; to her waist, to her hips, urging her against him. 'Why didn't you come and join me?'

Frissons of alarm surfaced, only to be ignored, outweighed by an answering need. 'I had no inclination to swim,' Rhiannon said faintly, puzzling over her extraordinary response to a complete stranger.

It occurred to her that she might be heading for trouble. Who was he? What was he doing here? The beach wasn't actually private, but as a general rule was used by hotel guests only. She pushed her hands against his chest, aware of cool, damp, hair-roughened skin, aware of superior muscular strength—but overriding this, aware of a powerful sexuality that under no circumstances could be denied.

He released her instantly, the merest frown visible, his smile reassuring. 'I'm frightening you? I'm sorry. It's just that I feel I know you already.' He traced the outline of her face with gentle finger-tips—her cheek-bones, the fine arch of her brows, her fractionally too large nose, the softness of her lips.

Rhiannon suffered his touch, forcing herself not to respond, even though every nerve in her body leapt. She looked away from his hypnotic eyes and saw the faint circle of a full moon, ready and waiting for the sun's final departure.

Was that the explanation for her behaviour? She'd heard a full moon did strange things to some people. But she was a sane, normal person, not given to flights of fancy or irrational behaviour. Was this irrational? Or was it simply a basic chemical reaction that could happen to anyone?

She moistened her lips and looked back at him. He was watching her. 'Did you win?' he asked softly, his lips curved upwards in a caring smile.

Her brow creased. 'Win?' How she wished he would move away! A war of nerves was going on inside her.

'You were obviously fighting a mental battle?'

Wryly she nodded.

'You were debating whether I was a sex maniac or a healthily sexy male?'

'Is there a difference?' she quipped, his flippancy putting her suddenly at ease.

'Oh, yes.' He cupped her face, his thumbs moving in a tantalising caress across her lips, his eyes also on her mouth. 'If I were a sex maniac I wouldn't be standing here like this. All I want is a kiss.'

He bent his head and she lifted hers, and the contact was explosive. Whether it was the romance of the night or because he was a mysterious stranger, Rhiannon did not know. But his kiss was like none other—gentle and yet insistent, erotic but not frightening, persuasive, experienced, seeking a response.

A few seconds only she hesitated before her hands slid around the smooth firmness of his back. His tongue probed and searched and she moved sensually against him, moaning softly in the back of her throat, freely returning his kisses.

It was unlike her to respond like this to a man she did not know, but it was like a coming together of kindred souls, as though this was the man she had been waiting for all her life.

He left her mouth and her head fell back as he burned a fierce trail down her throat. Pushing aside her shirt, he nibbled an achingly throbbing breast, and then suddenly she was free.

'This is all wrong,' he said gruffly. 'I want to spend time with you, get to know you, not rush you like this. Let me get dressed, then we'll sit and talk and you can tell me about yourself.'

'I'm sorry, I can't.' Rhiannon's face was pained. This was the first time in a good many years that she had met a man who genuinely interested her. 'I have to go. I've been here longer than I intended already.'

'But I will see you again?' He disappeared behind the rock against which she had been sitting—how ironic, thought Rhiannon, that she had chosen this very spot. And then he emerged again zipping up a pair of tight, patched jeans.

'I don't know,' she frowned. It was crazy, not like her at all—and yet there was something about him. She too would like to learn more. At least he was gentleman enough not to take advantage. There was no reason to be afraid.

'I'll be here tomorrow,' he smiled. 'Same time. If you don't come, I'll understand.' He scooped up his shirt and tossed it over his shoulder.

Rhiannon studied the carved beauty of his face, the straight nose, the jutting brows, the expressive eyes which looked black in this light but could be any colour, the wide mobile infinitely kissable mouth.

In the darkness he looked aloof, he looked hard and untouchable, ruthless even, and she had for a brief space seen this side of him. But for an instant only. A mutual desire had been born. Fires raged in him now as they did in her.

She smiled softly, stood on tiptoe and touched his lips with her own, then ran lightly across the sand without a backward glance.

It was not until she reached Yurena and the sanctity of her room that she allowed herself to think of him again. She took a deep breath and looked in the mirror. Her eyes widened. She looked—beautiful! And yet never in all her life had she considered herself anything other than plain.

Her shoulder-length auburn hair, tousled by her flight, framed her face attractively. Her green eyes were shining, her cheeks flushed, her parted lips soft and dark. There was an air of expectancy about her. She looked like a girl on the brink of falling in love.

Touching the tip of her tongue to her lips, she wondered what madness had invaded her. This was not the first man to kiss her. She had not reached the age of twenty-four without her fair share of boy-friends. And yet—he was different. He was all man, for one thing—mature, self-confident, arrogant even.

It was difficult to put an age to him, but she would guess in his mid-thirties. He spoke Spanish with the typical sing-song accent of a Canarian, and yet he hadn't looked a typical Spaniard. Or was it the half-light that had played tricks on her?

She looked forward to seeing him again, and that in itself was surprising, since she had deliberately cut all men out of her life and immersed herself in running the hotel.

There had been a reason for it. Even since her parents had won a small fortune on the football pools back home in England six years ago, she had been bombarded with proposals of marriage. Boys buzzed round her like bees round honey, and even Jonathan, whom she had thought herself in love with, had let her down, making plans for what they would do with the money she was sure to be given.

When her parents announced that they were think-ing of buying a small hotel in the Canary Islands, she had been all for it, and as excited as they when the time came to go. But men were the same the whole world over, she discovered. The nubile daughter of a couple of rich hoteliers was a prime target, and she got sick and fed up with rejecting their advances.

They had been on Cerrillo for only twelve months when her mother died, and Rhiannon and her father were devastated, talking about returning to England. But a hotel was something her mother had always wanted, and never been able to afford before their win, and they both knew she would wish them to carry on.

So Rhiannon took a hotel management course in London, her father meantime running the place with the help of a temporary manager, and now she was vir-tually in complete charge. Tony Howarth had lost some of the enthusiasm that had carried him and his wife through their first year and was content to let his daughter make all the decisions.

It suited Rhiannon, she was able to immerse herself in her work and forget about men and sex and marriage—until tonight. Stifled emotions flooded back with a vengeance, making her realise what she had missed these last years.

'Rhiannon?' A tap came on her door.

Her father! She clapped her hands to her cheeks. She had completely forgotten their nightly ritual of drinks on the balcony when she gave him a run-down on what had happened during the day. But if he saw her like this questions would be asked, ones she was not prepared to answer at this stage.

'I'm sorry, Daddy. Give me five minutes, I'm just about to take a shower.' And she needed one. She needed to wash that man right out of her hair, as the song went. There mustn't be one trace of him left when she joined her father.

Her five minutes stretched into ten. She stood beneath the cooling jets of water, letting them play over her skin as the unknown man's hands had earlier. It was like reliving those moments, and she quivered from head to toe.

Who was he? she asked herself for the hundredth time. Where had he come from? Their hotel was the only one on this unspoilt island, and he wasn't one of their guests.

When her parents had holidayed in the islands prior to deciding to make them their home, they were disappointed that tourism was taking over to such an extent that soon there would be nowhere left for a quiet, away-from-it-all holiday. Lanzarote, Tenerife, Gran Canaria, they were all the same, saturated with tourists.

Upon exploring the smaller islands they had discovered Cerrillo. It was so tiny not many people had heard of it, and Yurena, its single hotel, was up for sale! They

couldn't resist it, and had never regretted turning their
backs on England.

But somehow this man had found his way here. And
Rhiannon was glad! Glad! He had put a sparkle in her
eyes and a tingle in her veins, and she couldn't wait to
see him again.

When she finally joined her father she had stamped
on her feelings sufficiently, she hoped, that he would
not notice. Inside she was as tense as a coiled spring,
but on the surface as cool and assured as always.

'Sorry I'm late, Daddy.' She dropped a kiss on his
brow and sank on to a cushioned seat beside him.

Tony Howarth was a small spare man who spoke
loudly and quickly and wore a pair of gold-rimmed
spectacles which he constantly pushed up the bridge of
his nose.

'Nothing wrong, I hope?' He sipped his Scotch and
frowned. It was unlike his daughter not to be punc-
tual, and he worried about her. Running the hotel was
a time-consuming, responsible job and not one for
young shoulders. But she had insisted. He did not help
as much as he should because the novelty had worn
off, and if it hadn't been for Rhiannon he would have
gone back to England.

She helped herself to her usual gin and tonic, sipping it nonchalantly. 'Nothing at all,' she answered.
Nothing wrong, just something different; a shattering
of her calmly ordered world; a sudden penetrating of
her defences. Why wouldn't that man go out of her
mind? 'I took a longer walk than usual, that's why I'm
late.' And kissed a stranger! 'I didn't mean to worry
you.'

He smiled wryly. 'I can't help it. I'll always worry if
anyone's late again. Remember the day your mother
was late? I didn't worry then, I didn't think there was
any need. And look what happened. She was dead, and

I didn't know.' His voice shook. 'I think we ought to go back to England, Rhiannon. There are too many unhappy memories here.'

She caught his hand. 'Daddy, don't, please! I thought you were over it. It's been five years. And the hotel's doing well now. Mummy would be pleased.'

'You're right, of course,' he said tiredly, gulping down his whisky and pouring another. 'I'm getting old and maudlin. You must forgive me.'

'You're not old,' she denied at once. 'Fifty-one's nothing. You ought to get married again. I'm sure Mummy wouldn't want you to spend the rest of your life alone.'

'And if I did who would keep you company?' he derided. 'I don't entirely hold with this career woman business. It's a woman's place to get married and have babies. There's plenty of time for a career once you've raised them. If you don't watch it you'll be too late.'

'Are you trying to get rid of me?' mocked Rhiannon. Up until tonight she would have bitten his head off, marriage was not a part of her plans, but now she felt differently. It was early days, though, and the man was her secret. Nothing might come of it—on the other hand . . . Deliberately she pushed him out of her mind.

'Rhiannon, my love, I want you to be happy. That's all I ask in life. And if I might say so, you're looking particularly lovely tonight. Have you done your hair differently, or is that a new dress?'

Blessing the fact that he was never particularly observant, Rhiannon smiled. 'It's my hair—do you like it?' Not having time to wash and blow-dry it before their nightly talk, she had pinned it up on top of her head, but it was a style she wore often, and he had never commented before.

'It suits you,' he nodded, 'shows off your pretty face.'

Was she pretty? Was that how he saw her? Did the
man on the beach think she was pretty? She hoped so.
She hoped he was sufficiently attracted to come again,
and that it hadn't been merely talk. It would be awful
if she went tomorrow night and he wasn't there. What
a fool she would feel!

She could hear the sea whispering on the beach and
wished they were still out there, wished she hadn't
rushed away. Had he realised she was afraid? Afraid
of feelings she had kept rigidly locked away? Feelings
he had awoken with just one kiss?

That night Rhiannon lay in bed a long time thinking
about him, not drifting off to sleep until the early hours.
And the next day as she went about her work she wondered where he was and what he was doing. Was he
still on the island? Was he perhaps a relative of one of
the islanders? It was a likely answer. Most of the young
men had left to seek work in America, coming home
only on infrequent occasions. Perhaps he was here to
visit his family?

If his patched jeans were anything to go by he did
not look as though he had made his fortune, and would
probably have been as well off tending crops of
bananas or tomatoes right here on the island.

She wondered whether he knew who she was. Had
he known she was from the Yurena? He had said he
felt as though he knew her, and his first instinctive
anger when he discovered someone watching him had
quickly changed when he saw her face.

Her lips compressed and she felt a swift pang of disappointment. Surely this wasn't yet another man after
her because he thought she was a good bargain? The
hotel was doing well, but they were limited as to how
many guests they could take, and would certainly never
become millionaires. Most of her parents' capital had

been sunk in the venture and she and her father needed the revenue from the hotel.

With all her heart she hoped that the man was interested in her for no other reason than he found her attractive. She would ask him tonight, she would get things straight right from the start.

Never had a day seemed so long. She couldn't wait for the evening meal to finish and the guests disperse so that she felt free to take her customary walk.

Usually she slipped into something old and casual, but tonight she dressed in a mint-green cotton dress that complemented the colour of her eyes, adding a touch of mascara to her lashes and a hint of green shadow to her lids. That was all she needed. Her cheeks already held a rosy glow and her eyes were bright with expectation.

She could not contain her disappointment when she found the beach deserted. 'I shall be here,' he had said, sounding as though he meant it. And then she saw him, his dark head bobbing in the water, ploughing through the waves towards her.

Somehow she had not expected him to be swimming tonight, or she would have planned to join him. He lifted an arm and she waved in response and stood waiting for him to reach her.

He strode through the shallows, his brief red swimming trunks a vivid splash of colour against his deeply tanned skin.

The sun had not yet gone down and she saw his face clearly, tough and vital, with a determined jaw and clear blue eyes which encompassed her as physically as if he were touching her.

She felt her skin prickle, but her answering smile was hesitant.

'I'm glad you came.' He looked at her for a long heart-stopping second, his eyes intent and disturbing, and shivers of anticipation ran down her spine.

'I wanted to find out more about you,' she admitted huskily, and this was the truth, although probably not in quite the way he thought.

He walked up the beach and Rhiannon followed, watching as he picked up his towel. Muscles rippled beneath the satin smoothness of his skin. He was in perfect physical condition.

At length he dropped the towel and took her hands, his eyes searching her face. Her own were caught and held by his total magnetism and she felt herself turning to jelly. But before giving him the encouragement that he sought she must first find out the real reason for his wanting her friendship.

She smiled tremulously. 'I think we ought to introduce ourselves.'

'What's in a name?' he shrugged. 'It will make no difference to the way we feel.'

That was true, but she had to find out more about him.

'But if you insist, Pasqual Lorenzo Giminez.' He released her hands and gave a mock bow. 'And you are, I believe, Miss Rhiannon Howarth, daughter of the proprietor of Cerrillo's one and only hotel, more or less totally in charge since the unfortunate death of your mother.'

Rhiannon frowned, feeling a chill steal over her. So she had been right. The only difference between him and all the other men was that he set her pulses racing. It was disappointing to discover that her assets and not her personality were the attraction, but she was glad she had found out now rather than later, when it would have been harder to make the break.

'And your family live on Cerrillo?' she enquired coolly, moving a step or two away from him and looking out to sea, for once not impressed by the magnificence of the slowly sinking sun turning the water to molten gold.

'What makes you think that?'

She swung around, missing his frown, but seeing the puzzlement in his eyes. 'You'd be staying in the hotel if you weren't visiting relatives—or friends,' she added as an afterthought.

'And you think that is how I knew who you were—from my supposed family?'

She nodded.

'And because I already know, you suddenly don't like me any more. Why is that?'

It sounded stupid, put so bluntly, and Rhiannon decided to be totally honest. He deserved that at least. 'As you can see, I'm no raving beauty, and I never attracted the boys—until my parents won some money. Then I appeared to be a target for every get-rich-quick male in the vicinity. Even out here I've had more than my fair share of fortune-hunters.'

He smiled then. He had a wide easy smile that revealed even white teeth and made you want to smile back. 'Rhiannon, first of all let me assure you that you're far from being unattractive. Maybe you could make a little more of yourself, but it's all there. With that auburn hair and English rose complexion you must be the envy of all the Spanish señoritas! And secondly, I am not after your money. Come, you will see why.'

Hesitantly she took his outstretched hand, allowing him to lead her along the beach and up on to the headland. From here they looked down on Cerrillo's tiny harbour, and anchored out in the bay was an impressive white cabin cruiser, its gleaming paintwork tinged pink by the setting sun.

'That's yours?' She lifted puzzled eyes to his face.

His smile was very much in evidence again. 'Are you impressed?'

'I think so,' she admitted. 'Are you on holiday?' He had to be rich, owning something like this—and she had thought he was after her money!

'Sort of,' he shrugged. 'Would you like to come and see it properly? She's a beauty.'

Her lips twisted ruefully. 'I'd like to, but I can't—not now.' She glanced at her watch. 'In fact I ought to be heading back. My father's expecting me.'

'Oh!' He looked disappointed. 'Didn't you tell him you had a date?'

A date! The invitation had been extended so casually it couldn't possibly be called that. 'I didn't know whether you'd turn up,' she explained.

'Then you don't know me very well at all, my beautiful Rhiannon.' His breath was warm on her cheek, his arm firm about her waist. 'And you are beautiful,' he insisted when she opened her mouth to protest, 'also very desirable.'

Rhiannon closed her eyes as an impossible heat pervaded her. Beauty was in the eye of the beholder, so they said. Perhaps he did think her beautiful?

'Will your father be very worried if you don't return? You're not a child, you know. You are allowed a life of your own.'

'You don't understand,' she protested. 'Ever since my mother died he's always had this fear something's happened to me if I'm more than five minutes late.'

'She fell down the cliffs, I believe?' he prompted softly.

Rhiannon nodded. 'And lay there for over two hurs before anyone found her. How did you know?' She pulled out of his arms. His knowledge of her family was unhealthy.

'An English colleague of mine stayed at your hotel earlier this year. He got talking to your father and heard the whole sad story. When he knew I was visiting Cerrillo he told me about it.'

'That doesn't account for the fact that you knew me on sight,' she accused sharply.

'Rhiannon, stop being suspicious,' he said softly. 'Your photograph is in the hotel brochure.'

'And you've studied it sufficiently to recognise me even on a dark night? I could have been a hotel guest.'

'You could, but I'd been there earlier in the day.'

'You have all the answers,' she acceded, relaxing slowly and returning his smile. 'Forgive me for doubting you.'

'You had your reasons,' he said softly, his arm once again curving about her. 'I don't blame you. How about taking me to meet your father?'

Her eyes shot wide. She didn't want to share him with her father, not yet.

'You don't think that's a good idea?'

'It's a little—er—soon in our relationship, don't you think? I mean, I hardly know you. Why don't you tell me something about yourself?'

'All in good time,' he muttered, encircling her in his arms and urging her against him.

Fire coursed through Rhiannon and she dropped back her head and looked at him. The glowing sun reflected in the blue of his eyes, making them almost navy. His hair had dried and was much lighter than she thought, swept back like a lion's name and of a similar colour.

But he was nowhere as fierce as a lion. He was gentle, like a domestic cat, and she felt very safe in his arms. She smiled softly and he kissed her, his lips moving sensually over hers, the tip of his tongue tracing the outline of her mouth.

Emotions long since battened down struggled for freedom, clawing along her nerve-streams, causing an aching desire that was completely alien.

She sucked in much-needed air and let his mouth invade hers, her arms creeping behind his back, her hips grinding against his. His heart hammered loudly and her own echoed in unison, and she asked herself what was happening.

Never had she imagined she would respond like this to a man she scarcely knew. And whereas last night his advances had disturbed her, today she felt no fear. He had no ulterior motives. He liked her for herself alone.

His fingers slid slowly up her spine, feeling her, exploring her, and mingled in the luxuriant thickness of her hair moulding her head, holding it firm while his kisses ravaged her face.

Her stomach muscles contorted as she strove to remain calm. She felt like a teenager on the threshold of first love, instead of a mature woman of twenty-four. She wanted more, much more of what he had to offer, but it was not wise to run. She had to walk, to tread carefully, to make sure she was following the right track.

'Pasqual!' She eased her hands between them and pushed against his chest, liking the sound of his name on her tongue. 'Pasqual, I'm sorry, I must go.'

He stilled and then expelled a deep breath. 'Your father—you will allow me to come and meet him?'

What could she say? To refuse would be churlish. But did she want the two men to meet so soon? It seemed she had no choice. Already Pasqual was retracing their steps, his hand in hers, hurrying her along, allowing her no opportunity to demur.

'I think this is the most beautiful of all the Canary Islands,' he said. The sea and sky were now both shimmering red-gold, the mountain a mysterious green, the white houses hanging precariously on its side bathed in pink. 'I can understand your parents leaving England and choosing to live here. You say they won some money?'

Rhiannon nodded. 'They scooped a jackpot on the football pools, took a holiday in the islands and fell in love with them. What they didn't like was the commercialism. That's why they chose to settle here.'

'And there's a demand for the quiet life?'

'Oh, yes,' she returned enthusiastically. 'People come here for all sorts of reasons—young and old. Not everyone wants disco music blaring in their ears night after night. We run trips to the other islands, obviously, but our guests are usually glad to get back.'

He looked impressed. 'Seems like you've hit on a winner.'

'We think so,' she said. 'It was my mother's idea. It's sad that she never lived long enough to see the success it has become. It was a struggle to begin with. The previous owners had let it run down and when my parents first took over business wasn't very brisk. They'd had no experience in hotel management, you see, but I went back to London and took a course, and now it's going from strength to strength.'

'You're quite a girl,' he said, his eyes admiring, and Rhiannon preened herself under his gaze. He made her feel good, someone special, and she was glad she had met him.

CHAPTER TWO

TONY HOWARTH'S eyes widened when Pasqual followed Rhiannon on to their balcony. It was the first time she had invited anyone into their private quarters.

'Daddy, this is Pasqual Lorenzo Gimenez,' she said in English. Her father had never mastered Spanish and apart from a few necessary words he always used his mother tongue, whereas she spoke the language fluently. 'Pasqual, my father, Tony Howarth.'

Pasqual stepped forward and held out his hand. 'I'm very pleased to meet you, Señor Howarth, and I do hope that you'll pardon my intrusion?'

To Rhiannon's surprise his English was perfect. She had assumed that because he spoke to her in Spanish it was his own language.

'Any—er—friend—?' said Tony Howarth, with a quick look at Rhiannon, 'of my daughter's is welcome. Do sit down. I don't think I've seen you before. Are you staying here?' A frown creased his brow as he tried to remember.

Pasqual shook his head, smiling widely, and sank into one of the vacant chairs. 'My cruiser's in the harbour.'

Tony looked impressed. 'I see. Where are you from?'

He shrugged. 'My father and sister live in Las Palmas, but I tend to move about a lot.'

'You're not married?' asked the older man bluntly.

Again Pasqual smiled. 'No.' And Rhiannon realised that she had held her breath as she waited for his answer. It was a possibility that had occurred to her, but she had not found the right opportunity to ask.

How relaxed he looked! It was impossible to tell that he was a stranger in their midst. His long legs were outstretched, his hands tucked behind his head, and he smiled warmly at them both.

'I was pleased to hear that you'd made the islands your home, Señor Howarth. We Canarians are very proud of them. I expect you know they were dubbed the Fortunate Islands by the Romans, and I agree wholeheartedly with that title. I count myself very fortunate to live here.'

Rhiannon watched the pride on his face, his changing expressions, and felt a surge of something akin to love for this man who had so suddenly and so explosively walked into her life.

'Not so fortunate for me,' said the older man sadly. 'They robbed me of my wife. I'm thinking of going back to England.'

'Don't start that again,' said Rhiannon firmly. 'You've never been so well off, and I don't mean financially. Think of the weather, for one thing. Where else would you find a more or less constant temperature the whole year round? It's such a relaxing life, Daddy, and you know it, and you haven't had one hint of bronchitis since you've been here.' More and more often these days, though, she had to plead with him to stay. But he always gave in. Ever since she was little she had been able to twist him round her little finger.

An indulgent smile spread across Tony Howarth's face and he looked at Rhiannon fondly. 'How about offering your guest a drink?'

'I'm sorry,' she said immediately. 'What would you like?'

'Scotch on the rocks, I think,' said Pasqual, observing the bottle already on the table.

Thus putting himself into her father's good books, decided Rhiannon as she fetched another glass. It was her father's favourite tipple, and he often lamented the fact that he hadn't a drinking partner.

Before long the two men were talking as though they'd known each other all their lives, and Rhiannon sat back and watched.

There was a definite air of sophistication about Pasqual and an arrogance which amazingly did not offend. She wondered what he did for a living. He looked as though he could be tough and determined if the necessity arose.

When their eyes met, which was often, there was always a hint in his depths of the desire he felt, and his encompassing smile turned her insides to jelly.

Her father too looked more animated than he had in a long time, and it was obvious that Pasqual was doing him good.

They chatted well into the night, well past her father's usual bedtime, discussing at length the hotel trade in the islands, Pasqual showing just the right amount of interest to endear him to her father. In fact they got on so well that Tony Howarth invited him to join them for dinner the following evening.

Rhiannon felt pleased. Her father had not been the same since her mother died, and his talk about returning to England worried her. Now he looked more like his old self. Perhaps all he needed was someone like Pasqual to talk to. Someone who loved the islands and would convince him that going back home would be a mistake.

She accompanied Pasqual outside, and once they were alone he groaned and took her into her arms. 'I've wanted to do this all evening.'

'Me too,' she confessed, a riot of emotion racing through her. It felt right and natural clinging to his hard body, and she had no qualms about admitting how she felt.

'Oh, Rhiannon!' His mouth found hers, pouring out the hunger he had been forced to keep at bay.

Her heart pounded crazily and she returned kiss for kiss, arching ever closer, drinking of his mouth as though her life depended on it. His hands moulded her to him, feeling each curve of her slender body, sending fresh rivers of excitement coursing through her.

'I don't want to leave you,' he said hoarsely. 'Come back to my boat with me, Rhiannon.'

She touched her hands to his cheeks and looked wonderingly into the intense blue of his eyes, knowing what it was that he asked of her. What stroke of fate had brought them together? 'I'd like to, I really would,' she said softly, 'but we hardly know each other.'

'What is time?' he asked. 'It's irrelevant when two people feel as we do.'

'I'm not sure how you feel,' whispered Rhiannon. He desired her, yes, that was obvious, but was he simply after an affair? She wanted more than that. If there was such a thing as love at first sight this was it. And she did not want to spoil it by doing anything she might regret.

'I feel,' he answered slowly, 'that I've known you all my life. You are the girl I've been waiting for. I think, Rhiannon Howarth, that I love you.'

His voice vibrated emotion and Rhiannon felt as though a whole orchestra had sprung into life inside her head. These were the words she wanted to hear—and yet still she hesitated. 'How can you say that?' she protested huskily. 'How do you know I'm the sort of girl you want?' And yet didn't she feel the same about him?

'I know,' he returned confidently, and proceeded to kiss her again and again until she was left in no doubt as to his feelings.

'Now say you'll come with me,' he urged. His whole body trembled with unleashed passion, his hands tracing the curve of her spine, lingering over the mound of her hips and buttocks, possessing the fullness of her breasts.

'No, Pasqual,' she said quietly. 'It doesn't mean I don't want to.' She did, she did! Like crazy she wanted him. 'But I still think it's too soon.'

'And your father wouldn't approve, is that it?' There was the merest hardening of his voice.

She shook her head. 'Not at all. I'm old enough to please myself.' She pulled his head down and kissed him, letting him see that she was as eager as he for a deeper relationship. 'But let's get to know each other better first.'

He heaved a sigh and smiled ruefully. 'You're right, of course. I'm being selfish. But, Rhiannon, I want you so. I've never met a woman who's instantly turned my life upside down.'

And she had never met a man who had done the same to her. 'It will be fun finding out about each other,' she managed. 'How long will you be here?'

His lips twisted ruefully. 'No more than another day, two at the most.'

Rhiannon's heart grew heavy. So soon. He was going so soon. She had not expected this. 'Do you have to? Is your holiday over?' Why hadn't he come here earlier, then they could have had more time together?

'All good things come to an end,' he said sadly. 'So I'm afraid we haven't much time together.'

'But I will see you again?' she frowned. 'You won't just leave and that will be it?' She didn't think she could stand that; she had waited so long for someone like this.

'What do you think?' His smile sent fresh warmth cascading through her and he kissed her again, his mouth rougher this time, bruising her lips, his arms binding her as though he never wanted to let her go.

She felt the strong beat of his heart and clung to him too. He did not feel like a stranger. It was as though she had known him for all time, as though their coming together had been inevitable.

'I think,' she said slowly, when he eventually gave her a moment to breathe, 'that I shall be seeing quite a lot of you in the future, Señor Giminez.'

'And I think, Señorita Howarth, that you could be right.'

They clung for several more seconds, tasting each other's mouths, not hiding their need, but he did not again press her to join him. Instead, with an almost savage gesture, he pushed her from him. '*Buenas noches,* my love, I will see you tomorrow,' and he strode away into the blackness of the night.

The moon hung in the sky, silvering all it touched. It was a magical, romantic night, and Rhiannon looked after him until he disappeared. Then with a smile playing on her lips she walked slowly back to the hotel.

Her father was waiting up despite the lateness of the hour. She wished he had gone to bed; she wanted to be alone with her thoughts and her dreams.

'My darling Rhiannon, where did you find him?'

'On the beach,' she admitted sheepishly. 'Do you approve?'

'If you like him then I approve wholeheartedly,' he smiled. 'I'd given up on you. I thought you were destined to remain a spinster.'

'At my age?' she laughed. 'Give me a chance!'

'Your mother was nineteen when she married me, only twenty when you were born.'

'Mother found you, she was lucky,' said Rhiannon quietly. 'Pasqual's the first man who's been interested in me for myself, not because he thinks I'm rich.'

He laughed. 'You and your phobia! But he's a nice guy and I hope for your sake that something comes of it.'

Rhiannon shrugged. 'He's only here for another day.'

'And you think you won't see him again after that?'

'He says I will,' she smiled, 'but I don't intend counting on it.'

'You're wise,' he nodded. 'It doesn't do to be too sure. Has he told you much about himself?'

She shook her head. 'No more than he's told you. I wonder why?' Not that it mattered. Nothing mattered when they were alone, except the need to touch each other. That was all she wanted, Pasqual's hands on her, his mouth, their bodies pressed close. Even thinking about him twisted her stomach into knots.

'Daddy, would you mind if I went to bed? I'm very tired.' And she wanted to be alone. She had so much to think about.

'I'm tired too,' he acknowledged with a wry smile. 'But I've enjoyed this evening. I shall look forward to seeing your boy-friend again tomorrow.'

Her boy-friend! Pasqual was no boy. He was man, all man, and she had never met anyone like him. She grinned and went through to her bedroom, taking her usual nightly shower and then looking out of the window before getting into bed.

In the next bay, all alone on his boat, was Pasqual. What would have happened if she'd gone with him? Would they have made love? Would they even now be locked together in bed? Her whole body ached for him. Was he thinking about her too? Was he as tormented as she? Was this what falling in love was all about? Who could give her the answers? She wished she knew.

When morning came Rhiannon had slept little and went about her duties with only half a mind. All day she kept an eye open for Pasqual. He had been as reluctant as she to part last night. Surely he would try to see her before dinner?

When he did not turn up she felt hurt. Had he found another girl—one who was freer with her body? She suddenly discovered that jealousy was a painful emotion. Or was he exploring the island—alone? This was the most likely answer, she decided. Or at least the one that pleased her most.

She wore a blue and silver strapless dress for their dinner party, and told the chef they had invited a special guest. Normally whatever was on the menu was sent through to their private rooms, and it was always excellent, but she was taking no chances.

Her father looked at her appreciatively. 'Well, Rhiannon, if Pasqual wasn't bowled over before, he will be now. I don't think I've ever seen you so radiant.'

If the truth were known she felt good. Even her own mirror had told her she looked beautiful—for the first time in her life! If that was what being in love did, then it was something she would recommend to all the Plain Janes in the world. The effect was one which no beautician, however talented, could hope to achieve.

When Pasqual arrived he could not take his eyes off her, and she saw her father's satisfied smile. 'I've missed you, missed you terribly,' he whispered, as he held her for a brief moment, his lips formally touching her brow.

'Me too,' she breathed, her eyes wide and shining.

'I almost came this morning, but I knew you had work to do. It's been such a long day.'

She felt relief. Her suspicions had been for nothing. 'So what have you been doing?'

'Scrubbing the decks, swimming, watching the clock.'

Rhiannon grinned. 'Sounds a bit like my day. I was worried you wouldn't come.'

'Nothing could keep me away,' he assured her firmly.

The meal was excellent and the two men found plenty to talk about. And unlike the previous evening Tony Howarth retired early to bed.

'He must have guessed I wanted you to myself,' said Pasqual, drawing her responsive body close the instant her father left them.

'He approves of you,' she sighed, pulses racing, heartbeats quickening.

'And I approve of you—every delectable inch.' His hungry mouth claimed hers and Rhiannon's senses reeled. She felt dizzy with delight and desire and knew without a doubt that this was the man she wanted to spend the rest of her life with.

It was not infatuation, she was sure, nor just a chemical reaction. She loved Pasqual. She knew nothing about him—but it did not matter. This was the man for her.

He kissed her mouth, her eyes, her hair, the slender column of her throat and the satin-smoothness of her shoulders, and Rhiannon felt she was drowning in happiness. Her whole body ached with desire and she moved with unconscious sensuality against him.

He cupped her face and looked deep into her eyes. 'Rhiannon, can you take the day off tomorrow?'

'Yes,' she said, without even stopping to think. This would be his last day and she intended making the most of it. Besides, she hadn't had any time off for months.

'We'll go out on my cruiser and anchor where there's only the sky and the sea-birds for company. I don't want to share you with anyone, Rhiannon.'

It sounded a good idea to her too. 'Mmm, lovely,' she murmured. 'I'll ask our chef to pack a hamper and we'll just eat and talk and soak up the sun.'

'No need for food,' smiled Pasqual. 'I'm fully stocked and quite a good cook. But I can think of other things I'd like to do besides eat.' His mouth claimed hers again and his meaning was perfectly clear.

Rhiannon was not afraid—she wanted him with equal intensity. This was not a casual affair. He would come back.

They strolled down to the beach, their arms about each other's waists, her head against his shoulder. The sea was gentle, lapping the shore in soft undulating waves, unlike the riot of emotions struggling inside her.

In an odd sort of way she quite liked not knowing anything about Pasqual. It made him all the more mysterious, added spice to a relationship which was progressing at tremendous speed.

Conversely he knew almost everything about her. Her father had virtually given him the family history the evening before, and had even brought out old snapshots that made her want to run away and hide. Why wasn't she pretty like her mother had been? Why had she inherited her father's strong-boned face and determined chin?

But the pictures had apparently not put Pasqual off. He was still intent on seeing her at every opportunity. He stopped and pulled her in front of him, tracing the outline of her face with trembling fingers. 'I'm afraid, Rhiannon.'

Afraid? Pasqual? He was a tower of strength, in charge of any situation. What had he to be afraid of?

'I'm afraid of losing you,' he continued softly. 'It's all happened so quickly, it's too good to be true.'

'You won't lose me,' Rhiannon murmured huskily, shaking her head and looking into the blue of his eyes.

'I feel as you do. Unless—you change your mind?'

'Never! I want you for all time. I love you, Rhiannon, and whatever the future holds in store, for either of us, I want you to remember that.'

'I'm sure it holds nothing but happiness,' she said, wondering why he had said such a strange thing. 'I love you, too, Pasqual. I never imagined it was possible to fall in love so quickly, I've always scoffed at the idea of love at first sight. But now I know it can happen.'

He groaned and kissed her, devouring her lips. 'We're two lucky people,' he breathed, his arms crushing her against him, squeezing the breath from her body, forcing her to struggle for air.

'I think I'd better get you back,' he said raggedly, a crazed gleam in his eyes, 'before I tear that beautiful dress from your body. You drive me insane, do you know that? And I can't wait for tomorrow.'

His savage passion both alarmed and excited her. Should she back out? He was so much more experienced than she, he might want more of her than she could give. But she knew she would go. It was the best invitation she had had in a long time. And surely she was woman enough to handle him?

The next morning dawned cloudy and dull, but Rhiannon knew enough about the Canary Island weather to feel confident that very soon it would change to yet another shimmering hot day.

Her father's delight that she was taking a day off knew no bounds, and he instructed her to forget the hotel and return at whatever time she liked. 'Pasqual will look after you. I shan't worry.'

It was good to hear this, and Rhiannon dressed hastily in white shorts and a yellow strapless top, with her white bikini underneath. She popped a towel, her sunglasses, suncream, and a cotton jacket in case it was cool out at sea, into a bag and was ready.

Pasqual had offered to come and collect her, but she refused, and set out on her short walk with a spring in her step and a smile on her lips.

He stood at the rail waiting, and the moment she came into sight he leapt ashore and walked along the jutting stone pier to meet her. Rhiannon felt the now familiar excitement course through her limbs. How she was looking forward to this day!

They stopped and looked into each other's eyes, and she could not refrain from sliding her arms around him and lifting her face for his kiss.

He trembled and framed her face with his hands, taking in every detail, from the telltale pulse in her throat to the soft moistness of her lips and the love shining in her eyes. 'My Rhiannon, my beautiful seductress! Have you any idea how much your coming here today means to me?'

'I think I can guess,' she whispered. He was holding nothing back. All his desire and hunger and admiration were visible on his face. He loved her—as she loved him, and neither was making any attempt to hide it.

His kiss was tender and disappointingly brief, but when they climbed on board and he started the boat's engine her mind was quickly taken up with other things.

The cruiser was a dream of polished wood and shining brass, excellently equipped and luxuriously fitted. To think she had first thought he had no money! Owning such a boat must mean he was so wealthy that this was a mere drop in the ocean.

She was safe with Pasqual, safe enough to bask in the luxury of his adoration, safe enough to show the love she felt. Meeting him was like a dream come true. At last she could relax, be herself, have no fear that she was being used.

She inspected the boat; the neat galley and comfortable lounge, the four cabins and two bathrooms. Then she joined him at the tiller and looked out across the water, conscious of his strength and power at her side, proud that he had chosen her out of all the women he must know.

He smiled tenderly and they began to talk, to discuss their various likes and dislikes, their views about the islands, the weather, food. Everything and yet nothing, and time passed without them noticing it.

Pasqual dropped anchor and they lay on the deck and sunbathed, the sea all around them, the blue sky above them. And then they swam, diving overboard, playing and competing, laughing and joking, and Rhiannon had never felt so happy.

Soon it was time for lunch. She prepared salad while Pasqual cooked *cabrilla* he had caught early that morning. They ate the fish with chunks of crusty bread and washed it down with local white wine.

And then it was back on deck for more sunbathing. Rhiannon was enjoying every moment. He was a good companion, not demanding yet letting her know by a touch or a glance exactly how he felt.

The fact that he held back incited her to greater awareness, her senses at fever pitch when he finally made the first advance. She had thought him asleep as she lay looking at him, and gave a cry of surprise when he reached out and lightly traced a line down the length of her body, returning to cup one aching breast.

Rhiannon drew in a swift tortured breath and moistened her lips to accept his kiss. Her whole body throbbed and when he slid a hand beneath her she arched herself close, exulting in the feel of his firm muscled body next to hers.

Gone now was the lighthearted carefree mood that had tempered their morning. Pasqual was suddenly deadly serious. On the other hand he was in no hurry, kissing her one moment, merely looking at her the next, his fingers only lightly assaulting, skimming the soft curve of her waist, the length of her spine, tracing the mounds of her breasts, cupping her chin, tantalising, teasing, tormenting. Rhiannon felt she wanted to die. The blood pounded in her head, her heart clamoured painfully, and she ached for fulfilment. It was a slow seduction, and she was enjoying every prolonged minute of it.

Finally he could hold back no longer. His mouth claimed hers with savage fury, bruising her lips, pulling her roughly against him. The deck was hard beneath them, but neither noticed as their bodies twined and intertwined, hands and mouths joining, feeling, exploring.

In her previous relationships Rhiannon had always held something of herself back, but with this man she gave all. 'I love you,' she mouthed, her throat arched, his lips burning a fierce trail down its length.

'And I you,' he returned thickly, 'more than words can express.' His head moved lower, nudging aside the scrap of material that posed as a bikini top, hand and mouth possessing her breasts, kissing, sucking, biting.

Oh, the sweet torment of it all! Rhiannon moaned and groaned, her body writhing beneath him, her hands clawing his back, mingling in the wiry mane of hair, tugging and pulling, hurting him as he hurt her.

It was Pasqual who called a halt. Rhiannon was ready for the ultimate conclusion to their lovemaking. All sane reasoning had fled and she desperately wanted him.

'Rhiannon!' he groaned. 'We cannot go on. It is wrong. I cannot violate your trust in me.'

'But Pasqual, I want you, I need you—you can't let me down now!'

'You think I don't feel the same?' he muttered. 'Any othr girl and I wouldn't think twice. But I can't take your virginity.'

She glanced at him wide-eyed and whispered anxiously, 'How do you know I'm a virgin?'

He smiled. 'Your innocence, your shyness when it comes to making love, the way your reactions built up slowly at first, finally letting go with an abandon that both pleased and excited me. Anyone with experience would have let me see straight away what they were expecting. You're different and special, and that's why I love you.'

'I must be honest and admit it wasn't from choice,' she told him. 'I simply never met a man I loved enough to give myself to.'

'I'm glad,' he said gruffly, kissing her again, but less savagely this time.

She knew how much it cost him to hold back. His whole body trembled. But she admired his restraint and endeavoured to harness her own boiling emotions. Although at this precise moment she wanted him as desperately as he wanted her, she knew that later she might regret it. It was too early in their relationship for total submission.

Gradually they became still, their arms still locked about each other but their bodies no longer thrashing. Pasqual smoothed a strand of hair from across her cheek, smiling tenderly, and Rhiannon felt herself drowning in the navy depths of his eyes. 'Thirty-six hours is all I've known you, do you realise that?'

'A lifetime,' he murmured, kissing the tip of her nose.

'And I still don't know anything about you.'

'Will learning where I went to school or what I do for a living make any difference?'

'I suppose not,' she grinned. 'I love you because you're you.'

He crushed her to him. The unsteady beat of his heart throbbed against her breasts and she parted her lips for another deeply disturbing kiss.

When he had finished with her she ached from head to toe, her whole body alive and responsive and wanting him more than ever.

He stood up and pulled her to her feet. 'A cold shower's what we both need. I've never felt like this with any other woman, Rhiannon, and that's the truth.'

They stood together beneath the stinging jets, and it was a totally new experience, but perhaps a mistake. It did nothing to dampen her desire. Pasqual's hard cool body so close, hips and breasts touching, hearts still pounding, was sweet torture, and she was relieved if not pleased when he stepped out and left her to it.

She closed her eyes and stood there for several more seconds before finally joining him in the lounge. He had discarded his swimming trunks and pulled on cotton shorts, but there was still a smouldering intensity in his eyes, and she escaped into the nearest cabin to get dressed. It was safer this way. When naked flesh touched it ignited fires that were difficult to quench.

Once clothed she spent a few seconds brushing her hair and looking with interest at Pasqual's few personal belongings. His gold watch, a diary—had he penned in the day he met her?—a brochure he must have picked up from their hotel. Rhiannon smiled at his interest. A couple of paperbacks—both thrillers, a music cassette of *West Side Story*. These things told her far more about him than he had disclosed. Whenever she touched on his private life he changed the subject. She knew so little, and yet it didn't seem to matter. He would tell her when he was ready.

The sudden throb of the engine told her they were about to move, and she scuttled back up on deck.

Pasqual stood tall and straight at the wheel, and her heart burst with pride. This was her man, the good-looking, tawny-haired Canarian who had appeared out of nowhere and captured her heart.

'We're not going back yet?' she questioned with a slight frown. It was mid-afternoon and she had expected to spend the whole day with him.

'Of course not, but my hands are safer on this wheel,' he grinned. 'Come and stand here and tell me you love me.'

Rhiannon did so willingly, and stood with his arm about her shoulders, the ship nosing its way to nowhere in particular.

The rest of the day sped. Pasqual wanted to take her to a restaurant on Tenerife for dinner, but she insisted they stay and eat on the ship. She did not want to share these last hours with anyone.

All too soon darkness fell and it was time for him to take her home. 'When will I see you again?' She was afraid there were tears in her voice.

He looked at her tenderly. 'A couple of weeks. Think you can last that long? I shall be very busy catching up on work, etc., after my—er—break, so I might not have time to ring. But I will be with you in thoughts, don't ever forget that.' His kiss was savage, his eyes sad.

'Won't you come in and say goodbye to Daddy?' she ventured, trying to prolong this final moment of parting.

'It's late,' he said. 'I imagine he's in bed. Goodnight, my sweet love. Think of me a little. I'll be back just as soon as I can.'

He turned and was gone, and Rhiannon's steps were light as she entered the hotel. Her father was fast asleep when she peeped into his room. She smiled contentedly and was soon in bed herself. But her mind was too active for sleep.

She was loved and in love. It was the headiest feeling in the world, and she didn't know how she would survive the days until Pasqual returned. She wished he had given her an address so that she could write, and she could not help wondering why he was so reticent about himself. Not that it was important, but it would be nice to know something about him. Next time he came she would insist he tell her all.

Time went so slowly it was unbelievable, and after only a few days Rhiannon willingly accepted an invitation from an old friend of her mother's to accompany her on a trip to Tenerife. Marion came over every year from England for her two weeks' annual holiday, but Rhiannon was normally too busy to join her on her excursions. Sometimes her father did, sometimes Marion went alone, but this year it was just the antidote Rhiannon needed. The tension of waiting was unbearable.

Marion was in her early fifties but looked forty, with blue-rinsed hair and a still trim figure, and she and Rhiannon got on as though they were the same generation. They took a coach tour of the island, which was not the sort of thing Rhiannon usually enjoyed, but it pleased the other woman, and it was a convenient way of sightseeing. They finished their day with dinner at a hotel that had recently opened, but which had made such an impact with its publicity that Rhiannon had promised herself to come over and see it.

PLG International Hotels was a big name catering for people who liked plenty of entertainment, and she always found it interesting to see how other people ran things.

It was indeed impressive, but as expected had none of the intimacy that was so much a part of Yurena. Yurena's guests always felt that they were a member of the family. Here you had no identity. Nevertheless she could not fault the service or the food, and Marion was thoroughly enjoying herself.

'This is a marvellous place,' said the older woman, looking about her with interest. 'Haven't you ever thought of developing Yurena along similar lines?'

'Marion!' exclaimed Rhiannon, silently shuddering at how closely the tables were packed together, at the steady hum of over a hundred voices. 'If Mummy could hear you now she'd send you straight back to England!'

The older woman laughed. 'I wouldn't have dared say it to her, but I must admit I do sometimes feel Cerrillo's a teeny bit quiet. Don't you find it dull?'

'Not in the least,' answered Rhiannon. 'Daddy keeps saying he'd like to go back to England, but I wouldn't live anywhere else.'

It was not until they stood up to go that Rhiannon caught sight of a pair of broad shoulders and a tawny head of hair weaving through a sea of people towards the door.fftWithquickened heartbeats she hurried to catch him up. What was Pasqual doing here? Why hadn't he told her so that they could have met?

'Rhiannon, where are you going?' Marion's voice called after her, but she ploughed forward, then came to a sudden halt as she saw he was not alone.

A slim, exquisitely dressed dark girl was at his side, and as he handed her into a waiting car Rhiannon saw the perfect beauty of her face. She was younger than Pasqual, but very poised and confident, and even as Rhiannon watched the girl laughed up into his face and touched his arm with an action that spoke of a long-standing friendship.

For a minute jealousy cut through Rhiannon like a knife, then common sense prevailed. There was some perfectly logical explanation. The girl was perhaps a colleague. He was here on business. She must not jump to hasty, and probably entirely wrong, conclusions. He had said he loved her and she believed him, and the next time she saw him she would ask who the girl was. Meanwhile she would put the brunette out of her mind.

But a week later came the letter that smashed every single hope of happiness. She saw her father's face at breakfast as he pulled the sheet of paper from its envelope.

'We've had a take-over bid,' he said.

'And not the first,' she returned quickly. 'Tell whoever it is to get lost.'

'I think,' he said slowly, 'that this is one we can't ignore.'

Rhiannon frowned at his serious expression and took the letter from his hand. It was, surprisingly, from PLG International, but it was not so much what it said that drained the colour from her face, even though the offer was more than generous, but the signature at the bottom. Whatever she had expected it was not the name of the man she loved.

CHAPTER THREE

RHIANNON stared disbelievingly at the sheet of paper. It took several long seconds for it to sink in. PLG. Pasqual Lorenzo Giminez. He was PLG International!

It cleared up the mystery as to why he had been in that hotel in Tenerife, and it also told her in no uncertain terms that he had never had any real interest in herself. It was Yurena he was after, and she was willing to bet that the girl was no business colleague either, as she had naïvely first thought, probably only one of many girl-friends he had throughout the world.

To think she had fallen so readily and completely in love with him, and had been especially pleased at the long conversations he'd had with her father when she was busy in the kitchen! It had been lovely seeing them get on so well together, but never had she dreamt they were cooking up something like this.

'You knew this was going to happen?' she accused, her green eyes flashing, high colour staining her cheeks. She had never felt more furious in her life. Pasqual had obviously thought that if he got her on his side she would raise no objections. She had been unashamedly used—and after all the vows she had made to herself. For years she had been careful to keep the wolves at bay. And now this one, the biggest of them all, had slipped through a crack in her defence and caused devastating damage. She would never forgive him, ever.

Tony Howarth hung his head guiltily. 'You know I've wanted to go back to England ever since your mother died.'

'To what?' demanded Rhiannon. 'All the family you have is Uncle Frank, and he's as poor as a church mouse. He'll sponge off you, can't you see that? When you first won the money he was round like a shot. Prior to that you hadn't seen him in years. You're far better off here.'

'If you marry Pasqual I doubt I shall see much of you,' he said quietly.

'Marry him?' she gasped. 'I wouldn't touch him with a bargepole! He used me, Daddy. He knew you'd sell. You made no secret of the fact that you weren't happy, but he didn't want to take the risk that I might persuade you to change your mind. Tell him what he can do with his offer!' She was so angry she couldn't keep a limb still, curling and uncurling her fingers, pacing up and down, taking deep breaths and expelling them loudly.

'Oh, Rhiannon,' said her father sadly, 'I'm sure you have it wrong. The fact that he wants to buy this place is incidental.'

'If I told you I saw him with another woman the day Marion and I went to Tenerife, would you still think he felt anything for me?' demanded Rhiannon. 'I didn't say anything because I tried not to attach much importance to it. But it's as clear now as the nose on my face that all he's done is use me.'

'The girl could have been anybody,' said her father softly. 'There's no crime in him talking to someone else. You're behaving most unreasonably. I shall make a handsome profit and naturally give you half. You'll be a very rich woman.'

Rhiannon shook her head wildly, her auburn hair as fiery as her mood. 'I don't want money, I want to stay here. I want to run it the way Mummy wanted it. She'd never forgive you if she knew what you were contemplating. We had offers when she was alive, you know that, and she always treated them with the contempt they deserved.'

'They were never this generous,' he pointed out.

Rhiannon sniffed indelicately. 'If you really want to sell there's nothing I can do to stop you, but I'll never approve.' Her lips clamped and her face grew mutinous.

'Eat your breakfast,' he said gently. 'We'll discuss it again tonight when you've had time to cool down. I realise it's come as a big surprise. Maybe I should have told you.'

She glared. 'Both you and Pasqual knew I wouldn't agree. I don't know why you encouraged him.' Except that she had done the same thing in a totally different way. Icy shivers raced down her spine when she recalled how blatantly she had responded, almost throwing herself at him. What a fool she had been!

'I like Pasqual, he's a fine man,' persisted her father, his eyes sad.

'Hmph!' scoffed Rhiannon. 'Let's not talk about him any more.' She bit savagely into her croissant and afterwards attempted to carry on with her daily routine. But her heart was not in it, and in the end she delegated most of her jobs and went for a walk.

She avoided the beach like the plague. Never would she be able to walk there again without recalling her memorable first meeting with Pasqual. Instead she climbed the mountain. She needed to wear herself out until she was too tired to even think.

Flame-red poppies nodded their heads in greeting, pink and white wild roses clambered over the hillside, but today they held no magic for Rhiannon. She was blind to their beauty, trudging upwards, not stopping until she reached the top.

The mountain was actually an extinct volcano, and she stood for a moment looking down inside the bare and desolate crater. It about summed up her own feelings.

With a despairing sigh she sank to the ground and pulled her knees up to her chin. How dared Pasqual treat her in this manner! Had he really thought that by winning her love she would willingly back her father's decision to sell the hotel?

It was no coincidence that they had met on the beach, she realised that now. He already knew her routine and was aware that she would be curious if anyone should swim in that particular spot. And he had made sure that she fell in love with him. He had treated her as though she were someone special, he had even told her he had never felt like this about anyone else! And what was worse, she had believed him, opening her heart and showing him that she returned his so-called love.

For hours she sat there, feeling no better as the minutes ticked by. In fact, the more she thought about what he had done the more insulted she felt, and by the time she returned to the hotel her temper was at boiling point.

Her father was anxiously looking out for her. 'Where have you been?' He pushed his gold-rimmed glasses up his nose in a characteristically worried gesture. 'I was about to send out a search party!'

Rhiannon would normally have been all apologies, but today she was annoyed with him as well. 'What's the matter, were you afraid I'd gone to find Pasqual without telling you?' She ignored his hurt expression at her sharp tone. 'If I knew where he was I would have done. I want to tell that man just what I think of him!' The letter had come from PLG's Las Palmas office, but they also had offices in most major cities throughout the world. He could be anywhere. It would be like looking for the proverbial needle in a haystack.

'You could have spoken to him if you'd stayed here,' reproved Tony Howarth.

Rhiannon's head jerked. 'He's been?' Don't say she had missed him!

'He phoned,' amended her father. 'He wanted to make sure I'd had his offer.'

'Did he?' Rhiannon's tone was highly sceptical. 'Or was it to find out what my reaction was? I hope you told him. Did he say where he was phoning from?'

'No, he didn't. But you won't have to wait long. He's coming next week for my answer.'

'I hope it's not going to be yes!' cried Rhiannon. 'I've never fallen out with you in my life, Daddy, but this is one thing over which we'll never see eye to eye. I won't forgive you if you sell to him. Just think what it will do. He'll change everything, he'll expand, he'll turn it into one of those horribly commercialised places which you and Mummy so abhorred. It will be hateful. You can't do this, I won't let you!'

'Rhiannon, calm down!' He attempted to touch her, but she swung away angrily. 'I've not said yes.'

'But you will, I know you will. You've been after a way out ever since Mummy died. You don't care about me.' There was a break in her voice as she faced him, not really stopping to think what she said, conscious only of a searing anger inside her that seemed as though it would never go away.

'When Pasqual and I discussed this he intimated that he had more than a passing interest in you,' he said patiently. 'I felt no need to worry.'

Rhiannon shook her head angrily. 'What a nerve! He never loved me. He tricked me. If you'd seen the girl he was with in Tenerife you'd know that I couldn't possibly be of any interest to him. She was beautiful, absolutely beautiful. I was a means to an end, that's all. He made me fall in love with him and then came up with this irresistible offer. Still, when all's said and done it's up to you. I'm going to my room. If anything urgent crops up you'll have to deal with it yourself.'

At any other time she would have hated herself for speaking to her parent like this, but as things stood she felt she had every right to be angry. Her father should never have discussed selling without consulting her first. Even though the hotel did strictly belong to him he had allowed her a free hand in running it. Didn't that count for anything?

She sat at her window, her foot tapping impatiently, her lips clamped, her eyes staring blindly into space. What would happen if her father did sell? Would he expect her to go back to England with him? The idea did not appeal in the slightest. She liked it here. The Canary Islands had an allure all of their own, not least the climate, and she could not visualise living anywhere else.

But by herself? She had been too busy running the hotel to make friends, close friends. There were acquaintances, but none she could turn to for help. She would have to find herself a job on one of the other islands she supposed. Unless she opened up another hotel on Cerrillo with her share of the money? But that would defeat the object.

Although Pasqual would ruin the island in any case. He wouldn't continue to run the hotel as it was now, despite the fact that he agreed they'd hit on the right formula. Guests felt at home here. They could relax, be themselves. There were no brash lights or loud music. It was a haven, a place where one could unwind, and they had built up a very good reputation. How long would he keep it like that?

'Damn Pasqual!' she muttered. Why did he have to interfere? Why had he chosen their particular hotel and this particular island? Why couldn't he have put up another hotel on Gran Canaria or Lanzarote where one more would make no difference? Cerrillo was unique, and if he was allowed to introduce his own particular brand of commercialism—night spots, discos, sports facilities—it would be ruined. They were all the wrong things for this island.

Rhiannon stayed in her room until the restaurant manager needed her to discuss the following day's menus, and was then caught up in her usual whirl of activity. But her heart was not in it, and when she joined her father for dinner he looked anxious.

'I never thought you'd react like this.'

She lifted her fine brows. 'What did you think—that I'd clap my hands and say, "Goody, goody, we're both going to be rich"? I'd rather work here than have money in a bank account. Money doesn't make you happy.'

'But enough of it helps,' he said quietly. 'I'll be able to retire and settle down and——'

'Be as miserable as hell,' she finished bitterly. 'Ever since Mummy died you've shown no interest in this place, I'll admit that, but is selling the answer? If you really want nothing to do with it then sell to me and just live here. I'll raise the money somehow. But for goodness' sake don't sell to PLG. In no time at all the island will be as horribly commericalised as all the others.'

'He promised me that wouldn't be the case,' said Tony Howarth slowly. 'He said nothing would change.'

Rhiannon's eyes narrowed disbelievingly. 'I can't accept that. This is nothing like any of their other hotels. I saw that new one in Tenerife, don't forget. It's easy to make empty promises, but you sell out and in a couple of years you'll see that I'm right.'

He sat quietly for a moment looking down at his hands, his fingers interlocked, his thumbs revolving around themselves. 'I appreciate all you're saying, Rhiannon, but once I've sold and gone back to England it won't really worry me what he does.'

'Meaning you've made up your mind?' She shot him a furious glance. Not one word she'd said had made any difference. She might as well have kept her mouth shut and let him get on with it.

He nodded sorrowfully.

'And how about me? What am I supposed to do? I shall be jobless, homeless, and——'

'With your qualifications you won't be out of work for long,' he interjected. 'You could even come back to England with me and we'll buy a nice place in the country.'

'No, thank you,' answered Rhiannon bitterly.

'You're being most unreasonable!' Anger began to show through. 'It's unlike you to be selfish. I'm sorry if what I'm doing doesn't meet with your approval, but you're a child no longer. You have your life to lead and I have mine. I've decided to go back to my home country. It's as simple as that.'

Rhiannon compressed her lips. 'I'm sorry, Daddy, I can't stay and discuss this any longer. You're selling—okay, I accept that, but I don't know yet what I'm going to do. I have to think about it.'

Her father's face was sad as she left the room, but he knew it was no use at this stage calling her back. She had to come to terms with it in her own time.

She left the hotel and trudged down to the beach. Earlier she had been so careful to avoid it, now she wanted to bring back that first meeting, she wanted to fuel the fire in her heart.

Never had she felt such anger. Never had she been treated so callously. Who did Pasqual think he was? If it hadn't been so annoying it would be funny that he thought her opinion counted.

Admittedly her father left all the decisions to her, and anyone could be forgiven for thinking that she was in complete charge, but on an important issue like this her view did not matter.

It was a discovery that surprised and disappointed her. If anyone had asked whether Tony Howarth would sell without consulting her she would have given a definite no. It just proved that her father didn't think her capable of making real decisions.

The week passed with annoying slowness; each minute, each hour, each day, serving to increase Rhiannon's outrage. The rift between herself and her father deepened, and this was something else she could not forgive Pasqual for. She had never in her life argued with her father, they had seen eye to eye on almost everything. But this was such a big issue that she could not back down. Nor did Tony Howarth, it seemed, have any intention of changing his mind.

Each day Rhiannon took an hour off after lunch to relax, sometimes lying out in the sun on their own private patio, or often relaxing on the bed in the cool of her room as the early afternoon heat could be intolerable.

On the day Pasqual arrived she was outside. She had shed her working clothes and wore a bright orange bikini, a startling contrast to the green and white cushioned lounger on which she lay.

She opened her eyes and there he was, looking calmly down, a smile gentling his lips, warmth softening his eyes. 'So there you are! I've looked everywhere for you. How are you, my love? Have you missed me?'

The nerve of the man! Rhiannon shot to her feet and glared, green eyes flashing, arms akimbo. 'I'll say I have! I've been waiting for——'

Her loud words were swiftly stemmed as he took her into his arms and possessed her mouth. It happened so quickly that she had no time to avoid him, and despite the hatred that festered she felt a rising response. But it was an alien part of her, a part over which she had no control, and all it served to do was increase her contempt and anger.

'Let me go, you brute!' she hissed against his mouth. 'What do you think you're playing at?'

He stepped back and frowned. 'Rhiannon?'

'Don't tell me you're surprised?' Fury flushed her face, and the sun flamed her hair. 'Did you really think I wouldn't mind? Hasn't my father said anything about how I feel?' she asked incredulously.

'I haven't seen your father. I've only just arrived,' he said pointedly.

'But you've spoken to him on the phone? Don't put on the confused act, Pasqual. You know what this is all about.'

She turned away, not wishing to look at him. Annoyingly she still found him attractive, still with that power to turn her limbs to jelly, to send her pulses scurrying and her heart hammering. She must ignore him, send him away, make sure they never met again— and quite possibly the only way to do this was to go back to England with her father.

'I presume the take-over,' he said, his tone quiet, 'but I can explain. I——'

She shook her head wildly. 'I don't want to hear your excuses and your lies! What you did is unforgivable. My father's in his room—I'll call him.'

Pasqual caught her arm as she walked away and pulled her against him. His eyes were hard now, he was even angrier than she was. 'Rhiannon, you're making a big mistake.' His fingers bit into her wrist. 'Listen to me, listen to what I have to say.'

'No!' she cried savagely. 'I want to hear no more of your smooth talk!' She tried to snatch free, but his grip tightened and pain shot up her arm.

'Let me assure you,' he said fiercely, 'that everything I ever said to you was true.'

'That it was love at first sight?' she scoffed, head flung back, eyes brilliant. 'That you've never met anyone else like me? What do you take me for, Pasqual, an idiot?'

'You're no fool,' he said, eyes narrowed warningly. 'You're hurt, that's all. You've misunderstood.'

'I understand only too well what you tried to do, but you were wasting your time. Neither the hotel nor any part of it is mine. I have no say in the matter. If my father wants to sell then that's his choice. You needn't have bothered with me.'

He caught her other arm and forced her to face him. 'Is that what you think—that I used you? I can't believe it. I love you, Rhiannon, and I thought you loved me. In two short weeks have you changed so much?'

She swallowed hard and wrenched free. 'I trusted you, the only man for a long time that I've let near—and what was it you were after? Not me, not my body, but the hotel. The stupid silly hotel! Well, you're welcome to it. If my father wants to sell then good luck to him. But he won't be happy in England, even though he thinks so at this moment. He made a home here, and you're trying to take it from him.'

He shook his head, his lips grim. 'A business, not a home, Rhiannon. He hasn't felt right since your mother died. He wants his own four walls, not a giant of a place where there are always strangers present. It's you who's making the mistake in trying to stop him.'

She whistled impatiently through her teeth. 'I've given up trying to make him see sense. But if things go wrong for him I trust you'll have it on your conscience for the rest of your life!' With that she swung away and stalked indoors.

But her escape was barred when she bumped into her father. 'I heard raised voices. What's going on?'

She eyed him angrily, then looked over her shoulder. Pasqual had followed and stood there, face impassive, shoulders squared.

When Tony Howarth saw the younger man he smiled and stepping round his daughter held out his hand.

Rhiannon took the opportunity to slip away, nausea gripping her stomach when she heard the warmth of her father's welcome. How could he? How could he let this man walk all over him?

But it was no business of hers; she must remember that. With her head high she went to her room, achingly wondering what the future held in store.

It was clear her father had no intention of changing his mind. His pleasure in seeing Pasqual was all the proof she needed. But it was difficult to accept. She had hoped, had indeed prayed, that when the moment came he would think again. Now she knew they had been futile hopes.

She showered off her tanning-oil and smoothed in body lotion, then slid a cotton sundress over her head ready for the afternoon's work. For the next two hours she was on the desk and as they were expecting a new influx of guests she would have no time to think about Pasqual.

He would probably be closeted with her father all afternoon, discussing details of the sale. The thought brought a choking lump to her throat and her face was set, her eyes over-bright, when she eventually made her way to the foyer.

In the middle of the hustle and bustle, the filling in of forms, the allocating of keys, the excited voices all clamouring for attention, she became aware of someone watching her.

She lifted her head and across the sea of people saw Pasqual. His blue eyes were fixed unnervingly upon her and she was trapped for a moment like an animal in a light-beam. His face was hard and impassive, but she was as aware of his thoughts as if he had spoken out loud. He wanted to speak to her—soon. He wanted to put himself back into her good books—though why, when he had got what he wanted, was a mystery.

Swallowing hard, she turned her attention back to their guests, but found it impossible to shut him from her mind. He could well have been standing next to her instead of the other side of the room, and it was annoying to find her pulses racing and a flush stealing up her neck and cheeks.

When finally all the guests had been dealt with Pasqual strode over to the desk. 'I want you to have dinner with me tonight.' There was no smile, no encouragement, just a plain statement of fact. He did not even look as though it would be a pleasurable experience.

Rhiannon raised her brows and eyed him coolly. 'No, thank you.'

'I want to talk to you.'

'I said no!'

'You're making a grave mistake.' His blue eyes were condemning.

'The mistake was yours,' she thrust. 'I see no point in continuing any sort of relationship. It was all pointless and a total waste of time.'

'Rhiannon.' He placed his hands on hers where they rested on the edge of the counter. 'Let's forget your father, forget this hotel, just concentrate on you and me.'

'Why?' she demanded, wanting to tug away but not wishing to give him the satisfaction of knowing what his touch did to her.

'You know why.' A sudden hard note entered his voice.

'All I know is I want nothing more to do with you!' she hissed, turning with relief to one of their guests who had come along with a query.

When the woman had gone Rhiannon continued, 'This is not the place to hold such a discussion. Will you please go.'

'Only if you promise to have dinner with me.'

'I always eat with my father,' she grated, green eyes defiant.

'Tony has already given his blessing.'

Silently she cursed her father. But there was a look in Pasqual's eyes that told her he would not go away until she agreed. 'If I come out with you tonight will you leave me alone afterwards?' she asked with a heavy sigh.

'If that is still your wish by the end of the evening, you have my word,' he said, smiling now, but it did not reach his eyes, and Rhiannon supposed she had to be satisfied with the arrangement. It looked as though it was the only way she was going to get him off her back.

But she made up her mind not to enjoy the evening. She would put up with Pasqual's company because she had no choice, but that was all. In fact she couldn't imagine why he was persisting, since he had already got what he wanted. Unless it was because he had had a taste of her body and wanted more before he gave her up altogether. He would be doomed to disappointment!

He turned up looking devastating in tailored white slacks and a white shirt with a faint blue stripe, and Rhiannon had to quell an unwitting response. But when he took her hands and raised them gallantly to his lips her cool smile belied the erratic racing of her pulses. 'Rhiannon, you are beautiful.'

And you're a liar, she thought. Did he really think flattery would help? 'I am what I am,' she said coldly. 'Shall we go?'

With the merest touch of his hand on her elbow they walked away from the hotel, but it was not to either of Cerrillo's restaurants that he took her, which was what she had expected. Instead he led the way to the harbour. 'I trust you've no objection to a meal on board my boat?'

'Would it make any difference?' she asked coolly, trying to hide her apprehension. This was going to be more difficult than she had anticipated. 'You've obviously made your plans.'

'I didn't foresee any problems,' he said, his eyes skimming her face.

Rhiannon shrugged and attempted to laugh, though it wasn't easy. 'So long as you don't expect me to do the cooking?'

'Everything's in hand. All I want is for you to enjoy yourself.'

He had to be joking! With clamped lips Rhiannon stepped on board, following Pasqual reluctantly down to the main cabin where the table was already laid.

It was as elegant as any restaurant with white table linen and gleaming silver. There were pink and silver flowers—and even pink candles waiting to be lit. She arched her fine brows. The scene was set—but for what? It looked as though she had made a grave mistake in accepting his invitation.

'You don't approve?' A faint frown grooved his brow and his back was rigid as he looked questioningly at her.

'It's very—intimate!' He had said he would leave her alone after tonight—if that was what she still wanted! But it looked as though he had gone to great lengths to make sure she did change her mind.

'A beautiful woman deserves the best treatment.'

'Don't try to flatter me!' she cried, thinking about the girl she had seen him with. 'You destroyed my trust in you. I'm not likely to give you a second chance.'

Pasqual's smile was slow, confident and sensual, his blue eyes smouldering. 'I can be very persuasive.'

Her eyes widened again. 'I don't doubt that, but forewarned is forearmed, so they say. And I have no intention of giving in to you.'

His eyes held hers for a couple more seconds, and excitement shot through her veins. His message was very clear. He wanted her, and by the end of the evening he was going to make sure that she wanted him!

He moved suddenly. 'Let's have a drink,' and his action brought her back to her senses.

'Perhaps a small sherry?' She mentally resolved not to let him ply her with alcohol. She needed to keep a clear head if she was to pit her wits against his.

'I have something much more interesting than sherry,' he announced, opening a cupboard which turned out to be a refrigerator stocked with drinks, and selecting a bottle of champagne.

Rhiannon looked at it doubtfully, knowing what this unaccustomed drink could do to her. 'I don't really think we have anything to celebrate.'

'I thought we had.'

'Maybe you have,' she thrust, 'but I'll never forgive Daddy for selling to you!' She watched as he expertly opened the bottle, giving a tiny cry when the cork shot out, ricocheting off the ceiling and landing almost at their feet.

Automatically she bent to pick it up, and when she straightened he had filled her glass. His fingers brushed hers as she took it, lingering for an instant, watching closely her reaction.

It was difficult contriving to remain cool and unaffected when his touch felt like a branding iron. But somehow she managed an indifferent glance, stepping to one side, determined to put several feet between them.

She missed his frown as she pretended interest in a print of a three-masted sailing barque, spinning on her heel when he said softly:

'To us. May the future hold everything we both desire.'

His glass was held aloft, his eyes glittering ominously, and Rhiannon felt a quiver of apprehension.

'To us,' she confirmed, 'although I doubt whether our paths will cross again.'

'Then your father hasn't told you?'

She frowned, a sudden cold shiver riding down her spine. 'Told me what?'

'That you're to stay on and run the hotel when PLG International takes over. I think, Rhiannon my love, that we shall be seeing quite a lot of each other in future.'

CHAPTER FOUR

'DADDY said I'd stay on—as part of the deal?'
Rhiannon stared at Pasqual aghast. It was unbelievable! Her father had no right. Why had he? He knew
her feelings where Pasqual was concerned. Had he
thought that if he compelled her to remain here she
would feel any differently?

She realised her father was fond of Pasqual—but to
push them together after the way he had tricked her
was diabolical.

'Tony agreed with me that as you know so much
about the hotel you would be the ideal person to run
it for PLG.' He spoke calmly and matter-of-factly, as
though there was nothing wrong in the arrangement.

'Didn't it occur to my father that I might not want
to?' she enquired coolly.

'He knows you don't want to go back to England,
that you'll have to find yourself another job, so why
not here where you've been happy?' He made it sound
as though it was the obvious thing to do, as though she
was an idiot for thinking anything else.

Rhiannon tossed her head, auburn hair flying, eyes
bright and aggressive. They were not going to tell her
what to do. If she had been approached about the matter, given the choice of saying yes or no, she might have
given it some thought—but to be confronted with a
cut-and-dried arrangement was asking too much.

'I was happy here with my parents, admittedly,' she
said. 'The hotel is a home as well as a business. But if
your company takes over it will change. I'd prefer to

find somewhere else to work, somewhere where there are no memories.' She jutted her chin and eyed him defiantly.

'In other words,' he grated, 'it's because of me?'

He was suddenly angry, and Rhiannon felt herself caught and held by his powerful eyes, and became aware of a magnetic pull towards him, but it wouldn't work. There was no point in thinking it would. He had done the damage, and it was best to forget there had ever been anything between them. 'That's right,' she snapped.

Pasqual swore loudly and crashed down his glass, taking hers too and snatching her hands. 'Two weeks ago you were declaring your love. I swear you'd have walked to the ends of the earth with me. I refuse to accept that you've changed your mind simply because I didn't disclose my plans for the hotel.'

With clenched teeth Rhiannon glared, desperately fighting the awareness his touch evoked. 'I'm afraid you'll have to.' At this moment she was too proud to admit that seeing him with another woman hurt as much as anything else. If he had simply made an offer for Yurena she might have accepted his word, but she couldn't forgive him for two-timing her as well.

He swore violently. 'Shall I tell you something, Rhiannon? Shall I tell you exactly why I made no mention of my interest in the hotel?'

She shrugged. He was going to tell her whether she wanted to hear it or not.

His eyes narrowed and his mouth firmed. 'Because— I didn't want to mix business with pleasure.'

Her chin lifted. 'That's stupid. Yurena might be in my father's name, but I run it, not him. It's as much a part of me as—as the nose on my face.'

He ignored her outburst. 'I was afraid of exactly the reaction I'm getting now, and there's no room in my

business life for the petty arguments of a spoilt little
girl.'

Rhiannon gasped. 'How dare you! You don't know
what you're talking about.'

'Oh, I think I do,' he said, an aggravating smile
playing on his lips. 'Your father denies you nothing.
You always have your own way. He knew you'd be
against him selling.'

'For his own good,' she protested vehemently.

His brows rose. 'And you think he shouldn't sell—
for your own good?'

With clamped lips Rhiannon turned away. Admittedly she did get her own way most of the time. Being
an only child she usually managed to get whatever she
wanted out of her father. But spoilt? Never! 'I think
you're being too personal,' she snapped.

'Really?' His lips curled cynically. 'Can you deny
that you'd have reacted any differently if you'd known
I was interested in the hotel?'

She refused to answer.

'You've a chip on your shoulder the size of Mount
Teide,' he continued harshly, 'and are convinced that
no man can be interested in you for yourself alone.
What else could I do but conduct my business with
your father?'

Rhiannon looked at the hard-faced stranger. This
was not the man she had fallen in love with. This man
was ruthless. He didn't care what methods he used to
get what he wanted. He might deny that dating her had
nothing to do with the sale, but she would never believe
him, not in a hundred years. He was so clever with
words that he could twist them around to suit himself
whenever he wanted.

'Tell me,' he insisted, 'how would you have reacted
if I'd told you in the first place that I wanted to buy
Yurena?'

'I'd have told you to get lost,' she rasped.

'Precisely. Now can you see why I kept the two sides of my life separate?'

'You made me fall in love with you,' she accused angrily.

'I don't recall using force?'

'No, you used something far more subtle. You used your sex appeal. I imagine not many girls resist when you set out to charm. I wonder how many business deals it's actually clinched? Quite a few, I guess.'

Pasqual shook his head savagely, his breath whistling through the air. 'My patience is already thin, Rhiannon, don't try it any further. I love you—doesn't that mean anything?'

'Love? What's love?' she screamed, feeling almost hysterical. He had brought her here virtually against her will and was professing to love her, when they both knew it was the most ludicrous lie of the year.

'You don't know the meaning of the word, Pasqual. Cast your mind back to the day we met and deny if you can that you changed your attitude once you realised who I was. One second you were ready to tear me off a strip for daring to watch you swim, the next you were all smiles and apologies and wanted to know why I hadn't joined you. Isn't that proof enough that it's who I was that counted?'

Rhiannon had never felt so outraged in her life, and wouldn't admit even to herself that her anger was self-defensive—that she was trying to cover up a desperate hurt. As well as saying that she was spoilt he had implied that she ought to grow up and learn to accept people at their face value. 'I demand that you take me home this instant!' she finished savagely.

A curious light blazed from his eyes and with a swiftness that took her by surprise he shot his hands from her wrists to her waist, and urged her inexorably towards him.

'It would appear, Rhiannon, that you've forgotten how well mated we are. I think a little reminder is called for.' His fingers crawled up her spine, moulding her firmly against the hard length of his body. There was no escape.

Rhiannon struggled fiercely, ignoring the treacherous waves that shot through her, determined he should not break down her fragile defences.

'Rhiannon!' He breathed her name hoarsely. 'Oh, my Rhiannon. Why don't you believe in me?' His hands reached her head, imprisoning it, holding it at such an angle that his mouth could touch her arched throat.

It took all her will-power not to let her arms creep around him, not to give herself up to the aching pleasure of the moment. Nevertheless her breathing grew ragged as he continued his assault, and when his lips finally claimed hers in a deliberately sensual kiss, she gave a strangled cry of satisfaction.

Her lips parted and she accepted his deepened kiss, still moaning softly, her eyes closed, not wanting to see the face of this man who was making her respond against her will. She was in heaven one moment and hell the next; one second swinging from a star, another plummeting to the depths.

It was a precarious situation, and she must be careful not to confuse this chemical reaction with love. It was difficult when there was only a thin dividing line between the two, but she knew that had she truly loved him doubt would never have entered into their relationship. She had simply mistaken physical attraction for the real thing.

'That's better.' His voice was thick in her ear. 'Now you feel more like the Rhiannon I met and fell in love with.' His arms tightened, crushing her against his pulsing body.

Rhiannon struggled fiercely. 'No, Pasqual!'

'It's no good fighting,' he said, holding her at arms's length, smiling slowly and cruelly and possessively. 'Your body says it all for you. But perhaps it is time to call a halt, before I lose altogether my appetite for food and seek nourishment of a more—carnal nature.'

Rhiannon bit back an angry denial. It had been a foolish mistake agreeing to dine with him, even more stupid to come here to his boat. She had invited trouble. She might have known he would be unable to keep his hands off her. Why hadn't she been strong and said no? She had found out at their first meeting that it was impossible to resist him.

She sat down at the table, regaining her breath, pretending to study the variety of hors d'oeuvres he offered—cooked meats, shell fish, various salads, sausages. They were a meal in themselves.

'You're not hungry?' he asked when she took only a tiny portion of tomato salad—Canary Island tomatoes were beautiful, large and sweet and always a favourite of hers.

'What do you think?' she cried. 'I never wanted to come in the first place.'

His lips firmed, but whatever his thoughts he kept them to himself, doing full justice to the food, while Rhiannon sat and watched and sipped her champagne.

When he had finished he cleared away the first course and produced an impressive paella full of prawns, mussels and shrimps, chicken and rabbit, as well as the usual peas and rice and red peppers, and without a word he spooned some on to Rhiannon's plate.

She glared and ignored it, and continued to sip from her glass. When it was empty he refilled it, draining the bottle, and she could not believe that they had drunk it all. No wonder her head felt light. And she had thought it lack of food!

'I'll open another.' Pasqual sprang to his feet before she could stop him but she vowed not to touch another drop.

Once the meal was over, though, Rhiannon found herself shamelessly wanting his advances. He had insisted that she sit beside him and his mouth was close to her ear, one arm across her shoulders, the other resting on her thigh, burning into her skin. And fool that she was, she was doing nothing to stop him.

'I don't believe you no longer love me.' He had got over his former anger and was once again the sensually distracting man she had first met. 'You've been responding to me all evening. It's only a matter of time before you come to your senses.'

Rhiannon's eyes shot wide. The nerve of him! And yet wasn't what he said true? Wouldn't she, in her present condition, give in before long?

'I wouldn't be so certain if I were you,' she jeered, wishing she hadn't drunk so much on an empty stomach. 'It will be my pleasure proving you wrong.'

'I don't intend that to happen.' His tongue touched her ear, probing, exploring, sending shivers of anticipation down her spine. She wanted to move away but couldn't, ensnared and held by his powerful arms. 'I want you, and I'm impatient for you,' he growled, his hand moving upwards from her thigh, sliding with indecent slowness over her stomach and breasts, pausing for only a moment to feel her responsive hardening, then moving to firmly cup her chin, forcing her to look into the hot blue of his eyes.

'I don't take kindly to playing games, Rhiannon.' Anger was beginning to grow again. 'You'll be mine in the end, so you may as well make things easy for yourself.' His lips touched hers, lightly, erotically, assaulting her senses, making her head spin and her limbs quiver. But she refused to submit.

He pulled her lower lip down with a merciless thumb, kissing the warm, moist softness within. Rhiannon's breathing grew ragged—and there was nothing she could do about it. He was winning; despite her firm rebuff, slow inch by slow inch he was capturing her body, penetrating her defences. Soon it would be too late. If she wanted to hang on to her pride she must stop him now.

But did she want to? Her pulses were racing, her blood pounding. Her body craved fulfilment, ignoring the messages her mind sent to it. She had lost control.

His hands were on her back now, urging her against him. His kisses were brutal in their urgency, drinking deeply of her mouth, telling her clearly that he would not let her go until she succumbed.

Rhiannon's arms finally slid around him, her fingers clawing, an anguished moan escaping her throat. No other man had aroused her like this, no other man had made her feel as though she were spiralling through space.

There was no fight left in her. Her body became pliant in his arms; hungering, aching, wanting, giving. Time was forgotten, sanity had flown. Her throat felt tight and dry, her body throbbed.

'Rhiannon, tell me you love me.' His voice was deep, his hands firm on either side of her face, his smouldering eyes pinning her.

She could not look away and a lump in her throat threatened to choke her. It would be so easy to admit to a love which at this moment felt very real. But later, when she had cooled down, what then? Would she still be angry with Pasqual for cheating her? Still doubtful?

Yes, yes, yes, cried the sane part of her mind, visions of the unknown girl floating before her eyes. He's devious and cunning and you'll never be able to trust him. Go, now, while your pride is intact.

Stay, stay, urged another more insistent voice. Take what he's offering and worry about the future later.

'You're using emotional blackmail, Pasqual,' she whispered at length. 'You're not being fair. At this moment I admit I feel—something—but once I leave here I shall regret anything foolish I say now.'

His eyes darkened furiously. 'Is it foolish to admit that you love me, when we both know that it's true? Heavens, Rhiannon, what do I have to do to make you see sense?'

'You could have tried being open with me from the beginning,' she blazed. 'Have you any idea at all how much you hurt me?'

'I had my reasons,' he thrust, 'which I've explained. I can't understand you, Rhiannon, I really can't. You're fighting yourself, do you know that?'

'Am I?' she demanded. 'It's funny, I thought I was fighting you.'

He thrashed a fist furiously into his palm. 'I can see I'm not going to get anywhere at the moment. Tell me, would it be too much to ask if you'd at least stay on to run the hotel?' His tone was heavily sarcastic.

It was asking for her life. But what choice had she? It would be a job until she found something else. She eyed him stonily. 'Only if you promise not to make a nuisance of yourself.'

His brows lifted. 'It all depends what you mean by a nuisance. I cannot guarantee that I won't look at you, or speak to you.'

Rhiannon shook her head angrily. 'That's not what I mean. I just want you to keep your hands off me!'

'Don't make it sound dirty,' he snarled, a muscle jerking furiously in his jaw. 'I cannot recall ever doing anything against your wishes.'

'How about just now?' she rasped. 'Wasn't that a prime example?'

His eyes narrowed. 'Forgive me if my memory's so short, but I'm sure I stopped the moment you asked.'

Rhiannon said no more, pushing herself up and marching through to the galley. She would wash up. She needed something to occupy her hands, otherwise she would hit him.

He let her get on with it, which increased her anger still further, and when she had finished he suggested they go back to the hotel.

They walked in silence, and Rhiannon felt sure that the reason Pasqual had made no attempt to even hold her hand was not because of what she had said, but because that now he had bought the hotel and she had agreed to run it, she was of no further use.

Resentment and bitterness raged. Rhiannon felt like telling Pasqual that she had changed her mind. But what would she gain, except the satisfaction of giving vent to her anger? She had to let him think she was reasonably happy with the situation, then she could take her time looking around for another job. The idea of being out of work and out of a home did not appeal. But she had to be sure it was the right job, that she would be content, and that the salary was acceptable.

It was at this juncture in her thoughts that she realised Pasqual had not mentioned how much he intended paying her. It was one thing deciding to stay on, quite another if the money wasn't satisfactory.

'About salary,' she said at once. 'I hope that——'

'You won't lose out,' he cut in, and mentioned a wage that far exceeded her expectations.

Rhiannon lifted her brows, a hard tone creeping into her voice. 'Such generosity!'

He frowned, brows jutting. 'PLG always pay well, that way we get the best out of our employees. I'm treating you the same as everyone else.'

And there she had it in stone cold fact. She was no different. She was now an employee of PLG and that was that. It was all over; the brief flare of passion, the avowal of love, the desire, the pleasure.

All that was left was the pain. His treatment hurt more than she cared to admit. But she would do her job and treat him as she would any employer—with respect, with politeness, with deference if necessary. But certainly not with love. She had worn her heart on her sleeve for the last time. From now on she would maintain an icy indifference, and hope he would keep away from Cerrillo as much as possible.

He did not even offer to see her father. He had accomplished all that he'd set out to do and was now anxious to leave. More than likely his dark beauty was waiting somewhere in the background. Jealousy rose like bile in her throat, and when he bade her goodnight it took all her self-control not to slap him across the face.

Her lips were still compressed when she joined her father in their sitting room.

'Back so early?' Tony Howarth frowned slightly as he saw the unhappiness in his daughter's eyes, pushing himself up from his chair and walking towards her. 'Has something gone wrong?'

'Not from Pasqual's point of view,' she answered bitterly. 'Everything's perfect. I expect you'll think so too. I've agreed to stay on and run this place.'

'You have?' A broad smile widened his mouth. 'That's wonderful news!'

'But not much of a surprise?' she demanded. 'Wasn't it what you and Pasqual arranged?'

There was no mistaking the anger in her voice and he took her hands. 'Rhiannon, I'm sorry. It seemed the best solution.'

She grimaced. 'I must have been incredibly naïve to believe that he loved me.'

'So it's definitely all over between you?' Sadness shadowed his eyes and he pulled her gently into his arms. 'I think you're making a big mistake, Rhiannon.'

'It's easy for you to talk,' she protested, her voice muffled by his shoulder. 'He hasn't hurt you. I wish I didn't have to see him again.'

There was silence for a moment, then he said quietly, 'I'm afraid that will be unavoidable. The papers are signed. There's no backing out.'

Rhiannon jerked free. 'I didn't realise things had moved so quickly.' Something close to panic clutched at her heart.

'I saw no point in waiting,' said her father, his eyes apologetic. 'And I've booked my passage to England. I'm leaving on Wednesday.'

She closed her eyes, her heart suddenly heavy. Only one more day and she would be on her own. What a mistake it had been to immerse herself completely in her work! How she could do with a good friend now. Even Marion had gone back home.

Things moved rapidly after that. She saw no more of Pasqual, but as soon as her father had left, with a tearful farewell on both sides, representatives of PLG moved in. And apparently, despite Pasqual's opinion that they had hit on the right formula, it was felt there should be changes. They needed to attract a younger age group. It was too dull, too quiet, nothing to do. There should be tennis courts and a sailing club, a discotheque and a games room. The décor was too sober.

Rhiannon cringed as thoughts and ideas were tossed backwards and forwards. She was never consulted, treated as a mere employee, not the manageress, or the daughter of the previous owner. It meant nothing that for years she had run the place virtually single-handed.

An under-manager was brought in; young, small and slim, eager and over-enthusiastic, with bright fresh ideas and no knowledge of the requirements and needs of the type of person they catered for. He was all for new images, something bright and modern with plenty of life.

It came as a shock to Rhiannon when they were talking one day to discover that Miguel was the same age as herself. She felt so much older and definitely had a more mature outlook on life.

'People come here to get away from it all,' she insisted. 'The last thing they want is entertainment forced on them.'

'But it's so dull,' he complained. 'I really don't know how you stand it.'

Rhiannon eyed him defiantly. 'People make their own pleasure.'

'What pleasure do you get? I've never seen you go out—either by yourself or with anyone else. You can't convince me that you enjoy it here.'

That was because she was keeping an eye on her precious hotel. She still felt proprietorial towards it, and was ready to attack any outlandish suggestions that were made. But she could not tell Miguel this. He was 'on the other side'. 'I happen to like it here,' she defended. 'It's been my home for several years.'

'Your father owned it, I believe? Why did he sell? And why have you stayed on?' It was natural curiosity, nothing more, and Rhiannon knew she should not take offence, but she could not help feeling irritated by this young Spaniard's questions.

'My father wanted to go back to England. I didn't. It's as simple as that.'

'But did he have to sell? It must be difficult working in a place that once belonged to your family. Couldn't he have returned to his homeland and left you to run things here?'

'I'm sorry, Miguel,' said Rhiannon stiffly, 'I'd rather not discuss it.'

'Do forgive me,' he said at once. 'It's none of my business, I should not have questioned you. Let me take you out to dinner this evening to make amends.'

Rhiannon looked into the brown eyes regarding her so solemnly and surprised herself by agreeing. 'Thank you, Miguel. I think I'd like that.'

It would be the first time she had left the hotel since dining with Pasqual on his ship. She was long overdue an evening off, and could not imagine that either of them would be needed.

Several pairs of inquisitive eyes surveyed them as they ate their meal in a neighbouring restaurant, and it amused her to see the speculation, to guess at the way these people's minds were working. They could not be further off the mark.

Miguel was courteous and attentive without being too familiar, and despite her initial apprehension Rhiannon thoroughly enjoyed her evening. There was none of the excitement that tempered time spent with Pasqual, nevertheless Miguel was an entertaining companion. He had a mischievous sense of humour and she could see why he thought the hotel dull. It was certainly no place for a man of his disposition. She laughed more than she had in a long time. In fact it was almost a disappointment to go back to the hotel.

After that he often sought her out to share a joke or ask a question, and slowly Rhiannon began to realise what she had missed by shutting herself away on this island. She did not blame her parents, rather herself for remaining here when she could have lived in London or Madrid or any one of the world's lively capitals. And she also realised why she had been attracted to Pasqual. It need not have been him. It could have been any man. With his fabulous cruiser and exciting lifestyle she had seen a future of travel and luxury such as she had never tasted before. She felt foolish for being so easily impressed.

And then he returned. When the knock came on her sitting room door she expected Miguel—they had got into the habit of sharing a late evening drink together—and it was a shock to see Pasqual walk into the room—but typical of him to return unannounced!

Rhiannon's ready smile faded.

'You were expecting someone else?' His narrowed eyes took in the floaty chiffon dress, strapless and seductive, the green eyeshadow to match, the brightness to her eyes.

Pasqual himself wore light-weight slacks and a pastel shirt. He looked tired and strained, and she guessed he had just arrived.

'I would hardly dress like this if I wasn't.' Her tone was sharp and defensive, and she was cross with herself for feeling the pull of his magnetism. She had come to believe that he meant nothing to her—and now he was making a mockery of her feelings.

'I was hoping you'd dine with me. I have a meeting with my advisers first thing in the morning, and then I'm off again.'

Green eyes met blue. 'If I'd known I would have kept myself free,' she announced drily. 'Next time, let me know when you're coming.'

'Meaning you have no intention of cancelling your date? Who is he?'

'Does it have to be a man?'

He looked again at the smooth bareness of her shoulders, at the gossamer-like material brushing her breasts and skimming her hips, at the length of slender leg and at her dainty green sandals. 'It's a man—and you look as though you enjoy his company. Does he know about me?'

Rhiannon's body tingled as though every inch of flesh had been exposed to his all too keen eyes. She drew in a deep breath and held herself proudly. 'What is there to know? That you're the boss of this establishment? I imagine he's very much aware of that.'

'Damn you!' His teeth clenched and he glared. 'That's not what I mean at all, and you know it!'

Rhiannon smiled sweetly. 'Does he know that you and I were once—in love? Is that what you mean? Well, no, I don't believe I did tell him. It didn't seem important.'

He froze, his eyes coldly impaling her, and Rhiannon felt a shiver of fear. This was the ruthless side to Pasqual. It was this hard streak that had got him where he was. But it wasn't a side of him that she liked. 'So I'm a has-been now?' he rasped. 'You've met another man who sets your soul on fire, who has the pleasure of experiencing your soft, pliant, totally feminine body? Who is he, Rhiannon? I want to kill him!'

She tried to smile, even managed a strangled laugh. 'Really, Pasqual, aren't you over-dramatising? He's a friend, that's all. Not that I have to explain myself to you. Our affair was brief, but it's over. You have no claim on me now.'

A pulse jerked madly in his jaw, his fingers curled, and Rhiannon thought for a moment that he was going to attack her.

'I've done a lot of hard thinking this last week or so,' she said defensively. 'I realise that when I met you I was in danger of sticking in a rut. You helped me out, and I'm grateful, but it wasn't love.'

'And this other guy,' he demanded, eyes blazing, his whole body rigid, 'do you love him?'

'No, I don't love him,' she said, endeavouring to hide the alarm that tightened her stomach. 'But I enjoy his company. He's good fun.'

'Does he love you?' The words were spat at her through gritted teeth.

'I don't think so,' she frowned. 'It's not the sort of thing we've discussed.'

'Has he made love to you?'

Rhiannon's temper began to fray. Questions, questions, and to what end? Pasqual was seeing another woman, probably more than one, so why did it matter what she did? She was a free agent. He had used her and lost her. Didn't he realise that yet? 'I refuse to answer any more of these pointless questions!' she hissed. 'There's nothing further that you and I have to discuss. Please go.'

His eyes closed for a moment and he drew in a deep ragged breath before glaring fiercely at her. It was impossible to imagine that she had ever seen desire or smouldering passion. 'I think that gives me my answer,' he clipped. 'I'll go now, but I expect you to be present in the morning when the plans are discussed.'

'What's the point?' she demanded. 'I've heard enough to realise that they're going to destroy this place. I should have known you'd want to alter everything.'

'Nothing will be done without my approval,' he said firmly. 'I want you there, Rhiannon, at nine sharp.'

Rhiannon remained staring into space long after he had gone, wondering what the future held in store. If drastic changes were made to the hotel she could not stay. It had been a mistake to let Pasqual persuade her.

And what powers of persuasion he had used! Her cheeks burned as she recalled the occasion, and when Miguel came into the room some ten minutes later she had not moved.

'You look flushed,' he said, a frown on his dark handsome face. 'Is something wrong? Are you ill? Can I get you anything?'

She looked at Miguel dully, and could not help comparing him with Pasqual. This man was small and slight, with shiny black hair and an eager expression. But by no stretch of the imagination could he be described as sexy.

Pasqual on the other hand had a powerful physique that emanated sex appeal. His tawny hair and brilliant blue eyes made him different from most Canarians, and there was probably not one woman who wouldn't take a second look.

'I feel like a change,' she announced. 'How would you like to take me out?'

He grinned delightedly. 'It will be my pleasure.' He had invited her constantly ever since that first date, but always she had refused. She was quite happy to chat with him in the hotel and have drinks together here, but always kept everything on a strictly impersonal level. Miguel, she guessed, would not need much encouragement. She already knew by his words and gestures that he found her attractive.

As they left the hotel Rhiannon became aware of a tingling sensation down her spine, as though someone was watching. Pasqual? But when she turned she saw no one. Obviously her meeting with him had put her on edge. Why should he spy? He had looked as though he was ready to drop straight into bed.

Yet still the feeling persisted, and defiantly she tucked her arm into Miguel's, laughing into his face.

'I feel better already. Perhaps we ought to do this more often?'

And the delight in his eyes told her that he too thought it an excellent idea.

CHAPTER FIVE

RHIANNON woke the next morning with a sense of foreboding, and it took her a long time to drag herself out of bed. She lay looking at the cloudless blue sky, at the Canary palms and pines climbing the mountainside, the exotic blooms splashing careless colour.

How she wished her father hadn't left! Admittedly Cerrillo had its barren parts; which island in the Canaries didn't? But there was no comparison with England. Here there was peace and sun, golden beaches and warm blue water, fresh breezes of pure clean air and all the time in the world to do what you liked. She could not believe he would not miss it.

At a minute past nine she presented herself in the office. Pasqual sat at the desk she normally used and the three men sat facing him. When Rhiannon entered they stood and waited until she took the only vacant chair before sitting again themselves. Only Pasqual remained seated.

He glanced pointedly at his watch. 'Now we can begin.'

Rhiannon glared, and after a few seconds' silence in which he seemed to be waiting for an apology, he said, 'Right, José let's hear it.'

José, the senior of the three, immediately began to outline their plans, and the more Rhiannon heard the more outraged she became.

Not only did they suggest sports facilities and a disco, but they wanted to refurbish the whole hotel—give it a facelift, throw out all the traditional Spanish furniture, create a bright modern image, add an extension, encourage a whole different class of people.

Pasqual sat through the whole recital without saying a word, no expression on his face to indicate whether he agreed or not. Rhiannon watched him intently, alert for the lift of an eyebrow, the tug of a lip, approval or disapproval—but nothing.

When finally the spokesman had finished Pasqual asked the others whether they had anything to add. But they both shook their heads.

'I can see you've given it a great deal of thought.' Pasqual's elbows were on the desk, fingers interlocked, eyes surveying each of them in turn. 'And it's a very sound proposition—in fact an excellent one. I should like to compliment you on the hard work you've put in.'

Rhiannon almost choked, her face tomato-red, her eyes brilliant. How right she had been not to trust him! He had no intention of following in her parents' footsteps. He was going to turn it into exactly the same type of hotel as all the others in his group.

She opened her mouth to speak, but Pasqual held up his hand. There was a curious light in his blue eyes. He was enjoying the situation, she was sure, even though his mouth gave no indication of humour.

'But there is just one thing, gentlemen: you haven't followed my brief.'

Meaning there were even more of these atrocities? Rhiannon felt her temper boiling over and it was all she could do to hold her tongue.

'Señorita Howarth is having fits,' continued Pasqual, his eyes sparking a challenge. 'It was not my intention that we change this hotel so dramatically. The Howarths had a very good thing going, and I want to maintain it. There seems to be a call for somewhere quiet and relaxing with nothing more to do than swim or sunbathe or walk, or even make your own amusement. Music—yes, I think we could do with more music, but not a discotheque. Something gentle and soothing. And I certainly agree we should extend, but nothing modern and garish. I'd like it kept in the old Spanish style. How about you, Rhiannon? What are your opinions?'

She glared for a few seconds, not altogether sure how to take this complete about-face. She felt sure he had deliberately misled these men and given her a few days of hell while they theoretically pulled the place to pieces and rebuilt it. 'I agree with you,' she finally admitted, even though she would have preferred to have a blazing row.

Somehow she ignored his triumphant smile and continued quietly, 'We've turned away a considerable number of people this last year, so I suppose the idea of an extension is a valid one, so long as it's in keeping with the original building. I think it might also be beneficial to build a larger swimming pool—our guests seem to prefer the pool to the sea. And if you're going to accommodate more guests you'll need a bigger dining room and more facilities in the kitchen.'

He nodded, still with that cynical twist to his lips. 'Are you listening, gentlemen? This lady has first-hand experience, so she knows exactly what she's talking about.'

So why hadn't he asked her to collaborate with them in the first place? It would have saved both time and money.

They went into detail as to exactly what was required, and Rhiannon grew excited despite her initial misgivings and participated fully in the conversation.

But when the men left and she and Pasqual were alone, she deliberately let her anger surface. 'Why did you let me think you were going to turn this place into some vulgar modern hotel?'

'I found it amusing,' he said carelessly, his lips quirking as he studied her outraged face. 'Tit for tat, isn't that what you say in England? You hurt me, so I hurt you.'

'I had good reason for changing my mind,' she thrust.

'And now you're consoling yourself with Miguel?' His tone became accusing and harsh, his eyes darker than usual, hooded and mean, slicing right through her.

Rhiannon winced, feeling the full force of his sudden fury, and she was glad the desk was between them—otherwise she felt sure he would have attacked her. But it proved her intuition was correct; Pasqual had watched them leave the hotel last night. And he did not like it! But it served him right. It was a taste of what she had felt when she saw him with that other girl.

'Miguel's great fun,' she protested, eyeing him boldly. 'We have a lot of laughs. I suppose I should thank you for bringing him here.' There was more sincerity in her voice than she actually felt.

'I didn't employ him to entertain you, merely to help out now your father's gone,' he rasped.

'I was running it myself before he left,' she announced. 'I don't see what the difference is.'

'Then you'd have no objection if I moved Miguel elsewhere?' There was a sudden icy calm about him that was more frightening than his anger.

Their eyes met and held, his still hooded and difficult to read, her own wary and defensive. 'If we're to expand then I will certainly need help. The decision is, of course, yours.'

'But you'd rather he stayed?'

Rhiannon felt like screaming. He was deliberately trying to force an admission. Perhaps it would be amusing to let him think she really was interested in Miguel? He was being particularly unpleasant at this moment and she felt like saying something to hurt him.

'Obviously I'd prefer it,' she said, demurely looking down at her hands, though the thought of Miguel as a lover made her laugh. He was all right as a friend, but she felt nothing for him. His touch and his kisses left her cold. Unlike Pasqual. From the instant she met him her body had responded, and she guessed it always would.

Pasqual's reaction was even stronger than she expected. He slammed his hands down on the desk and pushed himself up, his face an ugly red, his eyes blazing. She instinctively stiffened and backed away, wondering what words of wrath were going to crash about her ears.

His mouth was grim, muscles moving in his jaw as he ground his teeth. 'I never thought you'd be so fickle, Rhiannon, and for the life of me I can't imagine what you see in him. But the truth of the matter is that he needs managerial experience, and there's nowhere else I can place him at the moment. Therefore, he unfortunately stays.'

Rhiannon smiled brightly, as though the news cheered her, when in fact it didn't make one scrap of difference. 'And you, I believe, are going?' Leaving her free to see as much of Miguel as she liked, or so he would assume.

There was a moment's silence before he spoke, a moment in which Rhiannon felt the full electric impact of his gaze. 'I'm sorry to disappoint you,' a malicious gleam entered his eyes, 'but I've changed my mind. I'm in need of a holiday and I can't think of a better place in which to spend it.'

Rhiannon stared in disbelief, her heart suddenly racing. It was impossible to visualise Pasqual enjoying a holiday here. He was too active by far, both physically and mentally.

'If you ask me,' she said, with an attempt at nonchalance, 'you'll be bored out of your mind within a couple of days.'

'Not if you keep me company.' He quirked a brow. 'It will be good experience for Miguel to take over the sole running of the hotel.'

She glared, then looked away quickly, unable to face the smouldering intensity in his eyes. 'I can't—it wouldn't be fair. Miguel hasn't learned enough yet.'

'Practical experience will be his teacher,' snarled Pasqual. 'What's wrong, can't you bear the thought of being parted from him?'

Rhiannon said nothing, knowing that silence would be her best ally

Pasqual hissed through his teeth and came round the desk towards her, his fingers curled, his eyes narrowed and threatening. 'I don't believe that you have any feelings for Miguel. He's not your type.'

His hands fell heavily on her shoulders and her first instinct was to knock them away. But he would expect that—and she did not want to give him the pleasure of a physical fight. So she stood her ground and eyed him aggressively, waiting to see what was going to happen next.

'Haven't you anything to say for yourself?' he demanded, his fingers bruising. 'Have you misled me? Do you make a play for every single man who comes your way and then complain that it's they who are after you? Tell me, Rhiannon!' He shook her furiously. 'Tell me I was a fool for falling in love with you!'

'You never loved me!' she riposted. 'You were simply amusing yourself at my expense while you conducted your business with my father!'

He froze, his eyes becoming glacial, nostrils flaring, his whole body poised. 'On what do you base that assumption, Rhiannon?' His stillness was more frightening than his anger.

'I was such a fool!' she cried. ' I really did believe in the beginning that you loved me.' Her eyes grew wide and brilliant and she wrenched herself free, standing a few feet away from him. 'Until I saw you—with another girl!'

His head jerked and he frowned, but before he could speak Rhiannon continued, 'I thought that would surprise you. She was very beautiful, far better looking than me, and was obviously deeply in love with you. She didn't look as though she was a new friend either. Is it a game you're playing with her too?'

She paused for breath, and Pasqual, his face by now a mixture of fury and disbelief, said strongly, 'Where was this?'

Rhiannon smiled humourlessly. 'Tenerife—your new hotel—I was dining there with a friend. I saw you and came after you—and there she was. I don't mind admitting it was like a slap in the face, but at least it opened my eyes as to what you're really like.'

It was clear by his expression that he remembered the occasion, but if she had thought he would deny there was anything between him and this girl she was disappointed. He swung away, his face blank, and Miguel chose that unfortunate moment to come into the office.

'Am I interrupting something?' He glanced awkwardly from one angry face to the other.

'Not at all,' said Pasqual easily. 'We'd just finished. She's all yours. Excuse me.'

Finished! Rhiannon felt indignant. He had told her nothing. She still didn't know what this girl meant to him. Not that she cared. It was all over between them; he could please himself what he did. She wanted nothing more to do with him.

Miguel pulled a rueful face as Pasqual went out. 'I'm sorry if I came in at a bad moment. Were you arguing about his plans for the hotel? I know it's no business of mine, he is the boss and all that, but——'

'The hotel had nothing to do with it,' said Rhiannon, trying to smile. 'Did you want to use the office? I'm going now anyway. If anyone should need me I'll be in my private quarters.'

He looked at though he would like to say something else but didn't dare, and his brow was creased as she left the room.

Rhiannon did not see Pasqual again that day, but she knew if he was serious about staying she would be unable to avoid him. Under the circumstances she was glad that she had told him what was wrong. There would be no more scenes now. Their relationship had ended.

But if the affair was over she could not banish him from her mind, and after a night spent tossing and turning and wishing him a thousand miles away she got up early and went for a walk.

Without realising which direction she had taken she found herself at the harbour. There sat Pasqual's boat in all its glory, gleaming white and bobbing proudly on the waves. She wondered whether he was on board or whether he had spent the night in the hotel. Not that it bothered her, she hastened to assure herself, but if he was on the cruiser and he saw her he might get the wrong idea.

Swiftly she turned and retraced her steps. It still hurt, the thought of him with another woman, and she wondered why he hadn't bothered to confirm or deny it.

Maybe he had felt there was no point, since she had actually caught in the act.

So engrossed was she in her thoughts that she did not see Pasqual approaching from the opposite direction, stopping only when she almost cannoned into him.

His eyes were narrowed and thoughtful. 'So it was you I saw from my window? I couldn't be sure. What brings you out this early? Couldn't you sleep?'

Rhiannon cursed her heart for hammering. She wasn't pleased to see him, so why did it react? 'That's what you'd like me to say, isn't it? But don't flatter yourself. I often take an early morning walk.'

'You've been down to the harbour. Were you hoping to see me?' There was an enigmatic gleam in his eye as he watched her face closely.

She tossed her head, her auburn hair flying. 'I think we said all that was needed yesterday. Just because I came this way it doesn't automatically mean I was trying to find you.'

'No?' His brows lifted. 'I thought you might have had a change of heart?' There was a heavy hint of sarcasm in his voice. He knew this was the last thing she would do.

'Never!' Her eyes were brilliant against the pale early morning sun.

He sighed heavily. 'I too have spent a sleepless night, Rhiannon. And I've reached a decision. I'm leaving.'

'You are?' Rhiannon smiled, but wondered why she didn't feel delirious. This was what she wanted, wasn't it?

He nodded.

'When? Now?'

His face hardened. 'Not at this precise moment, I still have a few things to finalise. Need you look so pleased?' There was a bitter edge to his voice as his eyes held hers.

'If you were in my shoes you'd be feeling pleased,' she retorted. 'What were you expecting, that I'd say I was sorry? You did what you thought you had to do. It was just my bad luck that I got hurt in the process. I shouldn't have been so gullible.'

'Will you have a goodbye drink with me?' he asked quietly, all the harshness gone out of his face. He looked hurt and sad, and Rhiannon felt a moment's compassion.

She nodded. 'Of course.' It would do no harm—and quite possibly it would be the last time she would ever see him

He took her arm and began to lead her towards the harbour. She frowned and hung back, having expected to return to the hotel.

'I thought we might have that drink on the boat,' he said, 'since I've some papers to pick.' He held up his hands in a mock gesture of submission. 'I promise not to touch you.'

Rhiannon shook her head, smiling weakly. It was wrong to go on distrusting him. 'I'm not afraid of you, Pasqual. I was surprised that's all.'

It was a short walk and they remained silent, his hand still on her arm, Rhiannon's pulses racing. She could smell the distinctive woody scent of his after-shave and guessed it would remind her of him always. It was a pity things had turned out this way. She had really thought he was one man she could love.

He helped her on board and she preceded him down to the galley. 'I hope you weren't thinking of a hard drink?' she said over her shoulder. 'It's a bit too early in the morning for that.'

'Coffee, then,' he said, 'I don't mind. You know where everything is. Put the pot on and I'll be down in a minute.'

Rhiannon looked about her as she worked, saddened to think that this was the last time she would be on this beautiful boat. She had spent some happy moments on it. Now they would be nothing more than memories, fading in time as Pasqual himself probably would.

She lit the stove and filled the pot—and then heard the sound of the ship's engine. Frowning, she looked through the tiny window and to her horror saw that they were beginning to move.

With a scream she leapt up the steps. 'Pasqual! Stop! What are you doing?'

He stood at the wheel, a broad grin splitting his face. 'We're going on a little holiday, my love. And thank you for playing right into my hands. You made it a lot easier than I expected.'

'You can't! How dare you! Take me back this instant!' Rhiannon was furious, her face almost as red as her hair, her eyes ablaze, her hands clawing at his on the wheel.'

'Calm down, I'm not going to hurt you.'

'You promised not to touch me!'

'Nor have I. Nor will I, if you don't want me to.'

He looked very pleased with himself, and Rhiannon wished she were a man so that she could flatten him. 'Why are you doing it? What are you hoping to gain?' she demanded.

'You'll find out,' he said cheerfully. 'Why don't you carry on with making the coffee? And I could do with something to eat. I'm ravenous!'

Rhiannon clenched her fists. 'Make it yourself, I'm not staying here!' She ran from him and almost made it over the side before he yanked her back, pulling her abruptly against him and looking long and hard into the hot green of her eyes, before finally dragging her back to the wheel. He kept one hand tight on her wrist as he corrected the ship's course. 'Don't try that again,' he grated, 'or I might not be so lenient!'

'I wonder what my father would say if he knew what was going on?' she challenged angrily. 'He thought you were such a gentleman!'

Again that wry twist to his mouth. 'Your father has given his full approval. In fact this was partly his idea.'

Rhiannon gasped, but before she could say anything he continued, 'He agrees with me that you're being unnecessarily stubborn. I spoke to him on the phone last night. He was anxious to know what sort of a reception I'd got. Like me, he was, to put it mildly, perturbed to hear about Miguel.'

'And so together you cooked up this devious plot?' She tried in vain to wrench free. 'You're insane, both of you! I demand that you take me back this instant!'

He chuckled wickedly. 'Struggle all you like, my little spitfire, it will make no difference. The only person you're upsetting is yourself.'

Rhiannon stamped her foot. 'I hate you! Just you wait—I'll make sure you pay for this. Kidnapping is a punishable offence.'

'Don't forget,' he mocked cheerfully, 'that your father's also involved. Do you wish to have him brought to justice as well?'

She glared at him as he continued.

'Your father might let you get away with murder Rhiannon, but not me. If you behave like a child I shall treat you like one.'

Their eyes met and held, Rhiannon's mutinous, Pasqual's warning. And then he smiled. 'How about that coffee?' he asked softly.

Rhiannon could cheerfully have hit him. He was so smug. He thought he was so clever. There had to be something she could do? She couldn't let him get way with this.

Fury raged as she made the coffee and buttered some rolls, and when she took the tray up she slammed it down in front of him. He raised his brows reprovingly, then looked at the solitary mug. 'You're not joining me?'

'No!' she said brusquely, and swinging away went and sat on the foredeck, her knees pulled up to her chin, her eyes staring sightlessly ahead. How long, she wondered, did he intend keeping her his prisoner? And what was she going to do for clothes? Had he thought of that?

Perhaps Miguel would report her missing? If he did then the police would mount a sea-and-air search. The thought cheered her and she strolled across to him. 'You think you're so clever. Hasn't it occurred to you that I might be reported missing? If there's a search we'll soon be found; and what sort of a cock-and-bull story will you spin then?'

I'm not that much of a fool,' he smiled imperturbably. 'I left a note for Miguel to the effect that we're taking a few days' holiday and I'm leaving him in sole charge.'

Rhiannon's happiness faded and she scowled. 'I don't think he's experienced enough.'

'He'll learn. What interests me more is how he'll react to us being together. Do you think he'll mind?' His lips quirked as though he was having difficulty in holding back a smile of sheer pleasure.

'You bastard!' Rhiannon turned away, itching to strike him, but knowing she dared not. She was completely at his mercy. There was no saying what he would do if she antagonised him too much.

Cerrillo was no more than a speck on the horizon now, and she stood watching until it disappeared altogether, her hands gripping the rail, her body taut with anger.

'Why don't you sit down?' suggested Pasqual softly. 'We'll be stopping at Las Palmas to do some shopping, but that's at least a couple of hours away, so you may as well relax.'

'With you? How can I?' she spat, but she moved once again to the foredeck and sat hunched against the side. Las Palmas? That was interesting. If she kept her wits about her maybe she would be able to slip away? But the idea was instantly abandoned. She had no money, not even enough for a phone call. No proof of her identity either, so it was no good going into a bank. Much as it grieved her to admit it, she was completely reliant on Pasqual.

She sat there fuming, not even bothering to look at him when he joined her some time later. 'How long is this going to last?' he asked quietely.

Rhiannon lifted her chin and looked at him, her eyes as hard and brilliant as emeralds. 'Until you take me home.'

'You're being childish again.' There was a slight edge to his voice. 'Did you sulk when your father wouldn't let you have your own way? Was that how you got round him? Well, let's make it clear right here and now that it won't wash with me. Snap out of your mood, or I'll give you the good hiding you should have had years ago.'

Rhiannon counted to ten and tried to smile, but her lips were stiff and her teeth clenched, and her eyes shot daggers.

He began talking about the hotel and his ideas for it. 'This is quite the most exciting of my adventures. If anyone had asked me whether a quiet little hotel on a virtually unknown island, with little or nothing in the way of entertainment, would be a winner, I'd have scoffed, and I would certainly never have considered incorporating such a place into my group.'

'Everyone's not alike,' said Rhiannon with an effort. 'There's a real need for places such as ours—I mean yours,' she amended bitterly. It was difficult to remember that Yurena now belonged to him.

'If you're right,' he said, 'and this time next year I should know, then I'll definitely be opening further hotels along the same lines. I must admit my first thoughts were to bring it into line with the rest of the group.'

'And what changed your mind?'

You,' he returned simply. 'You were so uptight, so convincing, so sure that what you were doing was the right thing, that I decided to give it a go.'

'I hope, for the sake of the hotel, that you don't have second thoughts,' she said. 'Not that I'll be there to see any alterations.'

His brows jagged into a frown.

Rhiannon smiled humourlessly. 'Surely you don't expect me to remain there for ever? I agreed because I had no choice, but as soon as I find something else I shall go.'

With an angry snarl he pushed himself up. 'It won't be long before we reach Gran Canaria. Make sure everything's tidy below will you?'

Indifferently Rhiannon collected his tray and went down to the galley, taking her time, rejoining him only when he began negotiating a berth at Santa Catalina Pier. She stood and watched as he expertly brought his boat in line with dozens of other pleasure and fishing craft, and she could not help admiring his expertise.

Not far away were the docks and the larger ships— Chinese and Greek freighters, Russian trawlers, Spanish mail boats, and others anchored further out waiting for a berth.

Across the street from the pier was Santa Catalina Park, an enormous outdoor café. 'We'll lunch and then shop,' said Pasqual. 'I know it's early, but I get irritable when I'm hungry.'

And that wasn't the only time, thought Rhiannon. But actually the sea air had made her hungry too, and she thoroughly enjoyed Rancho Canario—a rich vegetable soup, followed by grilled octopus, a favourite of hers, and chocolate mousse. They remained silent while they ate, and drinking her coffee afterwards Rhiannon watched the other customers.

There were sailors swigging beer, there were tourists with peeling noses sipping cheap whisky, and there were tough tanned oil-rig men, who worked off the African coast, relaxing in their native Las Palmas. Everyone was talking quickly and excitedly, laughing and joking, appreciating the sun, the food and the beer.

Rhiannon wished she was with a more congenial companion. What would these people say, she wondered, if they knew she was being held against her will? Dare she cry out and appeal for help? Or would they think it a lark and take no notice?

'If you've finished,' said Pasqual, interrupting her thoughts, 'we'll go and do our shopping. I know a perfect little boutique where you'll be able to get whatever you want. Select enough to last you several days, and don't forget a hat. You know what the sun's like.'

He seemed to have given up any attempt to be friendly, which suited her, but she still hadn't a clue as to why he was going to all this trouble. She could only presume that it was revenge. He was offended that she'd changed her mind about him and this was his way of punishing her.

The proprietress of the boutique was dark, statuesque and obviously a good friend of Pasqual's, kissing him warmly when they entered and only belatedly noticing Rhiannon. 'Who is this?' she demanded fiercely.

Had this women once been his lover? wondered
Rhiannon, feeling a stab of pain which surely couldn't
be jealousy. She was very beautiful even though
approaching forty, and she had eyes for no one except
Pasqual.

'This is Rhiannon, Colette,' he said with a smile, his
whole demeanour suddenly changing to one of relaxed
friendliness. 'She and I are cruising around the islands
and she needs some new holiday clothes.'

The woman looked once more at Rhiannon. 'Congratulations! It's the first holiday I've known Pasqual
take in a long time. He lives for his work, does this man.
You must be someone special?'

'Rhiannon is a very unique person,' said Pasqual,
'and like me, she hasn't had a holiday in years.'

Colette eyed her shrewdly and Rhiannon wondered
what she had read into that statement. 'You want to
impress our mutual friend?'

'Rhiannon doesn't need to impress me,' interjected
Pasqual. 'I know her better than she thinks. Let's get
on with it, Colette.' He walked along a row of decep-
tively simple cotton dresses, which Rhiannon imagined
would cost the earth, reaching out one here and there
and handing it nonchalantly to the tall black-haired
woman.

Several hours later Rhiannon owned a selection of
clothes that were nothing like she would have chosen
for herself, and yet suited her perfectly. She could not
deny that Pasqual had excellent taste.

Next they visited a chemist for toiletries and then,
loaded up with their parcels, they headed back to the
cruiser. Pasqual looked very pleased with himself.
'Now you can spend the afternoon sunbathing,' he told
her.

'Why not at Las Canteras?' suggested Rhiannon.
Las Canteras was the largest and busiest beach in Gran

Canaria and there was every chance that she would be able to lose him in the crowds. And surely she would be able to persuade someone to take her to Cerrillo? Once there it would be a simple matter to pay whatever he asked.

'Because I don't happen to think it would be a good idea.' He slanted her a speculative glance which suggested he knew exactly what she was thinking.

'I don't think it's a good idea you keeping me prisoner,' snapped Rhiannon. Who would have thought during those first idyllic days that they would end up like this?

'Was there ever a more delightful prison?' he suggested with a mocking smile. 'Whatever you ask for will be yours.'

'Except my freedom?' she blazed. 'I can't believe that my father is part and parcel of this heinous plot.'

'Tony happens to think you and I are eminently suited.'

'Huh!' sniffed Rhiannon. 'He's worried I'll get left on the shelf. Any man would do so far as he's concerned. Don't flatter yourself that you're someone special!'

The grip on her arm became pincer-like. 'You once thought I was, I'm positive, and you'll never convince me that you've changed your mind. You're just too damned obstinate to back down.'

Was that what this was all about? Did he really think that by imprisoning her and battering her defences he would find the captivated girl she had once been?

She drew herself up to her full height, her chin jutting. 'That's right. I object to being one of a long line. So you may as well give up this foolish idea and take me back to Cerrillo right now.'

His eyes caught hers, but his smile was humourless. 'I can be stubborn too, Rhiannon. If it's a battle of wills

I can assure you that I intend to win.'

She compressed her lips but said no more. She would never give in to a man she could not trust, a man who thought nothing of dating two girls at the same time. What sort of a fool did he take her for? He couldn't, or wouldn't, even give her an explanation.

Once on board she stowed their purchases while Pasqual started the engine, and by the time she had changed into one of her new bikinis and climbed back on deck they were out of the harbour and anchored.

Two mattresses were laid out and Pasqual was presumably getting himself changed. Rhiannon eyed them stormily. She did not relish the thought of being next to him—but what choice had she? With a resigned sigh she lay down and closed her eyes.

It was several minutes before she became conscious of him joining her, and she glanced hostilely across. His deep tan was enhanced by a pair of brief white swimming trunks, and the sight once again of his superbly muscled body shot traitorous quivers through her veins, telling her in no mean terms that she was not as immune to him as she tried to convince herself.

He raised reproving brows at her scowl, but said nothing, stretching out on his back and immediately closing his eyes. It was impossible now for Rhiannon to relax. Fully dressed and arguing she could ignore his sex appeal, but with inches only separating their almost naked bodies, it could not be done.

Constantly her eyes were drawn to his hair-roughened chest, his hard flat stomach and muscular thighs. The corners of his mouth curved, as though he was experiencing pleasant thoughts, and she turned away in disgust. He might find all this amusing, but she certainly didn't!

Picking up her bottle of suncream, she began rubbing it furiously into her legs and was trying to reach the middle of her back when Pasqual said, 'Why don't you let me do that?'

She glanced across. His hands were linked behind his head and an even deeper smile curved his lips.

'No, thanks, I can manage,' she said crossly, stretching her arm that bit further.

'But it looks very awkward. Allow me.' He sat up and took the bottle. 'Lie on your stomach.'

After only a brief inner struggle Rhiannon obeyed. There was no point in arguing. She buried her face in the circle of her arms and closed her eyes, but when he undid the clasp on her bikini and eased the straps over her shoulders she cried out in anger, 'What the devil do you think you're doing'

'You look as though you're used to topless sunbathing,' he said smoothly.

That wasn't the reason, she knew. He hadn't said anything the last time they were here. He just wanted to embarrass her. 'Not in front of you,' she snapped.

He sighed impatiently. 'Don't be a prude.'

'It's not prudery, I just wouldn't feel happy,' she retorted crossly.

'I won't force myself on you, Rhiannon, if that's what you're thinking. You should know me better than that.'

Against her will she lay back down, but his touch, though firm and gentle with no hint of sensuality, triggered off a chain reaction inside her. She wondered whether he guessed. He traced the curve of her spine and up again, circled each shoulder blade in turn, slid down to her waist and hips, his motions slow and deliberate, feeling her curves, her bone structure, her femininity.

Crazily she wanted to touch him too, to feel his hard sheathed muscles, the silken firmness of his skin. She wanted to thrill to his naked flesh against hers, and felt a flare of desire that was going to be difficult to stem.

CHAPTER SIX

YOUR'RE getting burnt.'

Pasqual's low voice confirmed what Rhiannon already knew. She had lain on her stomach far longer than she would normally have done. It had never bothered her before to sunbathe topless, and if their relationship had been different she probably wouldn't have minded now. But as things stood she couldn't face the thought of his eyes on her. His whole attitude had changed. He had brought her here for reasons which at this moment weren't entirely clear.

'Rhiannon!' He shook her roughly. 'Wake up!'

She stirred and without opening her eyes rolled over on to her back. If she couldn't see him looking at her then maybe she would not feel self-conscious. Then she felt the bottle of cream pushed into her hand. 'Will you, or shall I?'

Abruptly she sat up, her eyes wide as she looked at him, furious to find him grinning over her embarrassment. 'I'll do it,' she snapped, but it was impossible not to imagine his hands in place of her own, and unconsciously she ran the tip of her tongue across her lips. She knew the exquisite pleasure his fingertips could create, the torment, the desire! Oh, hell, how was she going to get through the next few days? Did he know what he was doing to her? Was it an intentional part of his punishment?

When she had finished she lay down again and closed her eyes, trying hard to ignore the fact that he was still watching her. But she was too conscious of him to relax and she wondered if this was going to set the stage for the whole journey—wherever they were going!

Finally he lay down, but when his thigh brushed hers as he turned she knew it was no accident.

'Do you remember, Rhiannon, the last time we lay here like this?'

Did she remember? How could she forget? He had given her the impression that she was someone special—and she had really thought it might lead to a more permanent relationship. How cruelly those hopes had been dashed. He probably treated every girl he met the same.

'I remember,' she said quietly.

'It could still be the same.'

And he could still play around with other women behind her back! 'I don't think so,' she snapped. 'Too much has happened since then.'

'Like the advent of Miguel? That was a mistake.' He sounded angry with himself—or was it with her?

'Miguel's a good friend,' she defended. 'He's loyal, and honest—which is more than I can say for you.' With a furious burst of energy she pushed herself up.

'Now where are you going?' frowned Pasqual.

'I've had enough,' she said. 'I'm going to take a shower—if you don't mind?'

But when she came out of the shower he was in her room. Rhiannon pulled the towel more tightly about her and lifted her brows. 'Forgive me if I'm wrong, but isn't this supposed to be my cabin?'

He leaned indolently against the door jamb. His hard body tanned a deep brown, his white swimming briefs hiding none of his masculinity. His body was in perfect shape and it was impossible not to be physically affected by him.

'Wasn't the conversation to your liking, that you had to rush away?' he jeered. 'What was it you didn't like me talking about—our past brief but highly satisfying affair? Or Miguel?' There was the merest hardening to his tone. 'I find it very difficult to believe that Miguel is your type.'

Rhiannon's chin jerked. 'You're not qualified to say what my type is.'

'Aren't I?' His brows rose and there was a mocking curve to his lips. 'I would say I was highly qualified.'

'Because you think *you're* my type?' she demanded, wishing her would leave. The cabin wasn't very big, but he was. Physically and spiritually. He seemed to fill it with his presence, making breathing difficult, if not impossible—and his almost naked body was a torment to her eyes.

'Right in one, he answered casually.

'You must be joking! My type would never make secret arrangements behind my back. Nor would he two-time me with another woman.' Her eyes were scornful. 'Oh, no, Pasqual, you're not my type at all. I thought you were, once, until I discovered the true you.'

He smiled. 'Does anyone ever truly know a person? We all have secret sides to us. We all at some time in our lives act and behave in a manner that shocks our nearest and dearest. You don't agree?'

She shook her head strongly. 'You're trying to make excuses for yourself.'

'I don't need excuses, Rhiannon. I behave as I want. People take me or leave me.'

'And are they given a choice?'

He grinned. 'Every time.'

'So where's mine?'

Your choice comes at the end of the day—or should I say holiday? Some people need a little help in making up their minds.'

'And you're convinced that you'll be able to persuade me to have an affair with you?'

'Did I say that?' His blue eyes widened, his brows rose. 'Dearest Rhiannon, all I'm trying to do is make you realise that Miguel is not the one for you. I should hate you to make a mess of your life.'

As if he hadn't already!

'Miguel is still a boy feeling his way in the world—you deserve better than that.'

'He's fun!' she protested.

'He's inexperienced.'

'He's considerate.'

'He's too anxious to please,' he derided.

Rhiannon turned away impatiently. 'You think you have an answer for everything!'

Pasqual smiled. 'I usually do.'

And she could not argue with that. She took a deep breath. 'Will you please go, so that I can get dressed.'

'What's wrong?' he chuckled. 'Don't you like the conversation?'

'Neither the conversation nor the company,' she said pointedly.

'Now that is a shame.' He was still smiling, completely unperturbed. 'The conversation we can change, yes. I don't particularly like talking about Miguel either. But me—well, I'm afraid you're stuck with me.'

She seethed and glared, and he laughed and left the room. Angrily she discarded the towel and pulled on a pair of soft pink embroidered briefs and matching bra. The fact that he had bought them made her feel like tossing them into the ocean, but common sense prevailed, and she could not deny that they made her feel good.

A pair of deeper pink cotton trousers emphasised her slender hips and neat bottom, and a lacy top gave tantalising glimpses of her curves beneath. Without exception Pasqual's choice o clothes was designed to set a man's pulses racing, and she hoped she would not have to spend too much time fighting him off.

But when she eventually emerged from her cabin he had a map spread out on the table and barely looked at her. 'Come and tell me where you'd like to go tomorrow—and I don't mean back to Cerrillo.'

White shorts replaced his swim-wear, and a white and navy shirt hid his muscular chest, but standing so close that their bodies almost touched she could still not ignore his raw sexuality. And he must know she was not immune.

'You've made all the decisions so far,' she said sharply. 'Why should tomorrow be any different?'

'Because this is your holiday as much as mine, or don't you see it that way, Rhiannon? Are you going to be on the defensive for the whole time?'

'Naturally,' she said tightly. 'You won't ever make me feel the same towards you again. I think you ought to give up. Now!'

'Won't I? I wouldn't be too sure of that.' With deceptive swiftness his hands slid possessively behind her, imprisoning her body, while his mouth found hers.

Rhiannon gasped as the first pangs of awareness shot through her and with a strength born of desperation she pushed her palms against his chest, thrashing her head from side to side to avoid his hungry mouth. 'Get away from me, Pasqual! Don't touch me. I hate you—do you know that? I hate you!'

His eyes glinted with amusement. 'Hate is the reverse side of the coin to love. So close that it's almost impossible to differentiate. I think, Rhiannon, that it's still love you feel.'

'No!' she said wildly, her green eyes flashing with jewel-like brilliance. 'I'll never love you again!'

'Does that mean I shall be forced to keep you a prisoner for ever?' He looked as though the idea appealed to him enormously. 'I think, if you'd relax, you will find that nothing has changed between us at all.' His mouth claimed hers again, and this time Rhiannon was lost in a world of sensation that she had thought gone for ever.

But still she felt the need to protest. 'Everything's changed,' she demurred, managing to pull away. He had two-timed her—she must never forget that, no matter how deep her feelings ran.

'Only in your mind.' His mouth tortured the sensitive area behind her ears.

'No, it's fact. You're not the person I thought, Pasqual.' He had proved that he could not be trusted.

He traced a course down her throat. 'I'm no different. I still want you. You still drug my senses like no other woman ever has.'

His mouth returned to hungrily claim hers, but there was no tenderness. It was a deliberate sensual assault that made desire run through her like quicksilver. Rhiannon knew she ought to resist, that all he wanted was her body—hadn't he just said that? And hadn't she had it proved to her beyond any shadow of doubt? Yet still her mouth opened willingly and eagerly under his.

The exploration was mutually enjoyable, and Rhiannon's loins ached with an agony of longing that frightened her. She moaned softly with the sheer pleasure of it all, while at the same time she knew it was madness to give in.

Nevertheless she drank deeply of his mouth, her fingers entwining urgently into the rich thickness of his hair, wanting to pull him ever closer. She wanted to melt into him, so deep was her arousal. This was how it had been in the beginning.

When the need for air eventually forced them apart Rhiannon's legs were trembling, her whole body felt weak, and her heart was banging fit to burst.

Pasqual's face was pale too and his hand shook when he raked his fingers through his hair. 'That was good, Rhiannon, and I needed it. Lord knows how much I needed it!'

Me too, she would have liked to say, but she had already given away too much. 'Don't think it's a taste of what's to come,' she said instead, though her voice held no conviction. It was as weak and shaky as her legs.

'I'm a born optimist,' he grinned. 'But I also know better than to push my luck. Once you've—er—calmed down, how about cooking supper? You'll find everything you need. Like a Boy Scout I've come well prepared.'

She could have hit him. He was treating the whole thing as a huge joke—and the trouble was she could no longer convince him that she was not interested. She had given herself away.

Her cheeks flamed as she grilled steak and washed salad, and before the meal was ready he was back down, opening a bottle of wine and pouring her a glass to sip while she cooked. Then he hovered, glass in hand, watching her every move.

Rhiannon's heart throbbed uncomfortably and the gravy went lumpy. Furiously she stirred, but it stuck to the bottom of the pan. As she turned down the flame the gas went out altogether, and as she reached for the lighter she sent her glass crashing to the floor.

'What's wrong,' taunted Pasqual, 'does my presence disturb you?'

'Of course not,' she snapped, bending to clear up the mess, 'it's just that I'm not used to gas—ouch!' A shard of glass pierced her finger and she jerked upright, eyeing the offending fragment balefully.

'Let me.' He reached for a first-aid kit and pulled out a pair of tweezers, but his touch was almost Rhiannon's undoing. It sent fresh quivers down her spine and it took all her willpower to stand still. He glanced at her and frowned. 'Am I hurting?'

'A little,' she murmured, hoping he believed her, but the amused curl to his lips told her otherwise.

During the meal she wished herself a thousand miles away. He was acting as though they were lovers, as though this holiday had been a mutual arrangement, not as if he were her captor. She lost count of the number of times she felt herself drowning in the drugging sensuality of his eyes—they rarely left her face. And his hand frequently touched hers across the table, no matter how often she snatched away.

She tried to convince herself that it was better this way, that it would be unbearable if they were at loggerheads the whole time, and yet if she didn't rebuff him she would end up in his bed. If she had to make a choice she knew which one would give her the most pleasure, but she also knew that in the end it would give her the most heartache.

'I think I'll go to my cabin,' she said, the minute they had finished eating and she had restored the galley to its usual good order. Not that she was tired or even intended getting into bed, she would probably read, but it was the only way she was going to get any peace.

'So that you can lie in bed and think of Miguel?' he jeered. 'Or is it simply to escape me?'

'Both!' she retorted smartly.

'How quickly you change. Or wasn't the lesson good enough?' He put a hand on the galley wall each side of

her where she stood, imprisoning her yet not touching
her. 'Ought we, my sexy friend, to continue it right here
and now?' His lips quirked. 'Maybe you have the best
idea? I could join you. In fact I cannot think of anything at this moment I would enjoy more. What do you
say?'

Rhiannon felt like a trapped animal. Her hands
sought the coolness of the wooden panelling behind her
and her eyes were wide green orbs of fear—or was it
excitement? She was afraid to meet his gaze because
she knew she would be lost. Even now her heart beat
an urgent tattoo and there was that increasingly familiar ache in her loins.

Although these were new feelings for Rhiannon, no
other man had ever affected her so disturbingly, she
could not help thinking about all the other girls who
had responded to him in exactly the same manner—
especially the dark beauty in Tenerife. There was simply no way any woman could resist him. He was
undeniably a most physical man. He had everything—
looks, sex appeal, personality, strength, all rolled into
one fantastic body—and he thought he could have any
woman!

It was clear now that this was what it was all about.
He was still sore because she had rejected him—and
no woman ever did that! How could she resist him? he
was thinking. How indeed? Telling herself she hated
him was no defence at all.

'I don't think it would be a good idea, having you
in my cabin,' she said, surprised to hear how breathless
her voice sounded. She could feel his body heat, his
warm breath on her cheek—he might as well have been
touching her, the way her body reacted. Every pulse
was pounding, every nerve-end sensitive to his slightest movement.

'I'll give you a choice,' he said softly. 'Either I come to you, or you join me on deck?' He moved closer, thigh brushing shivering thigh, her breasts teased by the hardness of his chest, his lips tantalising the trembling softness of her mouth. It wasn't a kiss, it was an assault of her senses, and did far more than an actual kiss. It was a taste of what could be hers—if she was willing!

From somewhere she must draw the reserves of strength to resist. What alarmed her was that this was only their first day on board. How much of this could she take before giving in? She shrank still further against the wall. 'I'll come up on deck.'

With a mocking laugh he pushed himself away. 'I thought you might say that.'

The evening was fraught with tension. By every movement and gesture Pasqual made her aware of him—and he knew exactly the reaction he was getting. He didn't demand any kisses, he did not even touch her, but he stood close as they watched the sun set in a spectacular fiery display, and he sat disturbingly near when they talked about the islands and the hotel and whatever else came into their minds.

Often there was less than a hair's breadth between them. He made love to her in all of the senses except touch. His eyes admired and flattered every inch of her, melting her bones and contracting her stomach, causing her whole body to ache with primeval hunger. His long tanned fingers stroked the edge of his chair and she could imagine them, even feel them on her hardened breasts. Was there ever more exquisite torture? She watched his mouth as he spoke, his lips, his tongue, and touched her own tongue to her lips in an unconsciously provocative gesture.

She was glad when it grew dark so that she could no longer see him so clearly, but even then the deep disturbing tones of his voice could not be ignored. How long, she wondered, before she could decently excuse herself and go to bed? Without him saying it was still too early and he would accompany her.

In the end it was Pasqual himself who put an end to her anguish. He rose and stretched. 'I think it's time to turn in, unless you'd like a nightcap?'

Rhiannon shook her head.

He smiled, as though expecting this answer, and kissing her gently on the brow he disappeared.

She could not believe her luck. But, although she wanted to be rid of him, when she went to bed herself she lay awake for a long time listening to the sounds of him moving.

It had been an evening of pleasant torture, if those were the right words. Though she doubted if any words could express the feelings he had driven through her.

Sleep was virtually impossible. How could her body respond to a man she hated, a man who had abducted her and was keeping her on board his ship against her will? The trouble was, he knew the power of his sex appeal. He knew exactly how to get a woman to respond to him—and it need not be her—it could be anyone.

It had been the height of foolishness to respond to him in the first place, she knew that now. It had been the start of all her heartache. He was after nothing more than an affair. She ought to have guessed the type of man he was right from the beginning. A man did not reach his age without getting married unless he was enjoying a good sex life and didn't need the trappings.

When she did finally sleep it was dreams that disturbed her thoughts, but not about Pasqual. Nightmarish dreams about her mother. Falling down a cliff was a terrible end for so gentle a person, and after seeing her mother's mutilated body Rhiannon had dreamt about it for weeks and months afterwards.

And now, in her disturbed state, that nightmare returned. She woke in a cold sweat to the sound of her own screams and saw a black shape silhouetted in the doorway.

A light snapped on, and she closed her eyes against the brilliance, unable to think where she was or who it was who stood watching her.

'It's all right.' Pasqual's calm voice pierced her fear and she felt the bed give as he sat on the edge. 'You were dreaming, that's all.'

She shook her head, her eyes still closed, glad of the company, forgetting for the moment all that had gone on between them. 'My mother's dead—she just lay there—and we never knew. We might have saved her. We should have searched. It was our fault she died!'

'You cannot blame yourself,' he said, gently taking her hand.

'And now my father's left the island. What if anything happens to him? I should have gone too. I shouldn't have let him go alone. It was selfish of me!' Her voice rose and she struggled to sit. 'I must go to him!'

'Rhiannon, calm yourself.' He put his arm comfortingly about her shoulders. 'You're worrying for nothing. Your father's perfectly all right.'

He sounded so convincing that he almost had her believing him. But he wasn't God. If her father did fall ill he couldn't prevent it. She was being irrational, though. Her dreams always did this to her. Her fertile imagination ran riot and she felt that all sorts of bad things were about to happen.

'Would you like a drink? Hot milk? Brandy? Anything?'

She shook her head and snuggled deeper against his chest. She felt surprisingly safe in his arms, her nightmare already almost a thing of the past. Usually it took her a long time to get over such a dream.

'Then I suggest you try and get back to sleep,' he said, settling her against the pillows. 'If you need me, just call. I'm not far away.'

The light went out and he was gone before she could detain him. Memories of her nightmare remained, but somehow they were not so bad now that she knew Pasqual would protect her. He was a different man, all the mockery and tormenting gone, she didn't even mind at this moment that she was his prisoner. She fell asleep again almost at once.

But in the dead of the night her nightmare returned, and once more Pasqual came into her cabin. 'Would you like me to stay with you for a while?' he asked, sheltering her trembling body in his arms.

'Please,' she agreed faintly, too upset to worry about him being so close.

He released her and she lay down, watching as he put out the light. There were no chairs in the tiny cabin and she assumed he would sit on the edge of the bed, but in the shadow she saw him throw off his robe and the next second he was in bed beside her.

'Pasqual!' She sat bolt upright, her mind suddenly very clear. She ought to have known he would take advantage of the situation. 'What the hell do you think you're doing?'

'Scared?' he mocked with a hint of his old cynicism. Then he smiled and said calmly, 'Don't worry, you're quite safe. You have nothing to fear. Go to sleep, there's a good girl,' and he turned his back.

To sleep—like this? How did he think that possible? Her nightmare was forgotten. The hardness of his naked body sent frissons of excitment through her limbs—far more dangerous than dreams. There would be no more sleep for her tonight.

For a long time she lay afraid to move, listening to the sound of his breathing, imagining what it would be like if things were different. If she were here of her own free will. It she weren't his prisoner but his girl-friend. She would be in his arms now, a willing and eager lover, giving and receiving, loving and enjoying.

When it eventually became apparent that he was remaining true to his word it gave her a whole new insight into Pasqual's character. He was not all bad. In her time of need he was completely honourable. She began to relax and finally fell asleep.

Again she dreamt, but this time it was about Pasqual. They were together on the beach and she lay in his arms, freely accepting and returning his kisses. There were no cross-currents between them, nothing but a beautiful friendship, and when he told her that he loved her she readily believed him. 'I love you too, Pasqual,' she said.

When she awoke it was daylight, and she had the bed to herself. She lay for a moment pondering on the events of the night. What an extraordinary man he was! It was almost impossible to believe that the Pasqual she knew had lain so close and not taken advantage.

She crept through to the bathroom and took a shower, dressing in a pair of brief yellow shorts with a matching bandeau top. Having all these new and different things to wear was like putting on someone else's clothes.

In the galley the coffee pot was on, though there was no sign of Pasqual, for which Rhiannon was thankful. Facing him this morning would be embarrassing.

Several cups of coffee later she decided he was avoiding her. But when she went up on deck Rhiannon discovered that he was not on board at all.

She gave a mental shrug and made herself comfortable on the deck. The heat of the sun was soporific, or was it her disturbed night? Whatever, her eyes closed and she slept, and the next thing she heard was the throb of the boat's engines.

Pasqual was back, and they were heading—where? Jumping to her feet, she made her way aft and found him at the helm.

'So, the Sleeping Beauty has awoken at last,' he commented derisively. 'I'd begun to think you were going to sleep all day. How are you? No more nightmares?'

She shook her head. 'I suppose I should—er—thank you for keeping me company. I haven't had that dream in a long time. I can't think why it happened now.'

'It was my pleasure.' He gave a secret smile and looked so happy about the situation that Rhiannon wondered whether her dream about him hadn't been a dream at all. What if he really had kissed her. What if she had actually said that she loved him? Had she been admiring his restraint for nothing? Hot colour crept up her cheeks and she swung away.

'I've bought some fresh rolls for breakfast,' he informed her. 'I'm sure you must be hungry? I know I am.'

Rhiannon breathed again. She had   worrying for nothing. He would never have spoken so matter-of-factly if anything like that had happened. But it was a relief to escape, and she took her time preparing the rolls and making fresh coffee.

They ate their breakfast in the sun, and Rhiannon wondered if she was imagining the subtle difference in his attitude. Had last night given him false hopes? Had she, in her sleep, given something away? It was a disturbing thought and it made her determined not to let him anywhere near her again.

She washed up and returned to the deck, and he checked her as she walked past him. 'How would you like to take a turn at the wheel?' he asked.

Rhiannon eyed him suspiciously. Pasqual didn't normally make suggestions unless he had a motive. 'Why do you ask? I don't know anything about boats, and I'm not particularly interested.'

'I don't want you to be bored,' he said logically, his eyes perfectly innocent. 'It will be a whole new experience.'

As if meeting him hadn't been experience enough! But she shrugged. If that was really all he was trying to do it might not be a bad idea. 'Okay, what do I do?'

She listened attentively while he explained the controls, but surely it wasn't necessary for him to stand so close? Had he any idea at all what he was doing to her? How could she concentrate? 'But actually all you need concern yourself with at the moment is steering,' he said, his hand on the wheel beside hers. 'See that island?'

Following the line of his finger, Rhiannon spotted a purple mound in the distance, but she was far more conscious of his body touching hers than any obscure spot on the horizon. Had she guessed correctly and this was another ploy for him to get near her? Had last night given him the wrong idea? It had left her so vividly aware of his body that her skin prickled whenever he brushed against her.

'That's Tenerife. Head for it and give me a call when we're within a mile or so. There's nothing between here and there that need worry you.'

'Then why can't you set the automatic rudder?' Rhiannon edged a few inches away, hoping he could not hear her panic-stricken heart.

His hand covered hers on the wheel. 'Because I prefer not to. What's wrong? You look like a scared jack-rabbit! It's not difficult.' But as was happening far too often, his eyes were amused. He knew exactly why she was nervous. Rhiannon felt like telling him to move, but that would confirm what, after all, might be purely speculation—and might even make him increase his efforts. It was a game to him—she was different because she had rejected him—and he didn't care that she was finding the pressure increasingly difficult to bear.

He remained at her side for several more minutes, their eyes scanning the Atlantic together. Rhiannon constantly shifted position, but still he did not move.

Then his hand tightened and she wondered what was coming next. It was a relief when he said, 'I think you have the idea now. Shout out if you need me.'

He went below, and Rhiannon concentrated on steering the cruiser. It was a beautiful boat, and easy to control, but her attention was not fully on it. Still she could not push Pasqual out of her mind. Her whole body was as tense as a coiled spring and she was as conscious of him as if he were still by her side.

Fortunately he stayed below, and when Tenerife finally loomed close enough for her to call him she judged by his languorous expression that he'd been asleep. It was her fault he'd had a bad night, but so had she, and she did not feel the slightest bit guilty. She was hating him more and more, her feelings fired by her unwilling responses to his sexy body.

'You've done a good job,' he said, taking the wheel. 'Congratulations.'

She made sure their hands did not touch, moving quickly to avoid his intense blue gaze. 'It was easy,' she murmured.

She flung herself down in the sun as far away from him as possible, musing how long this enforced holiday would last. She was getting so mixed up in her feelings, one minute hating him and the next so intently aware of his charismatic charm that she wondered

whether she was still in love after all. Was that his aim?
Did he intend making her fall for him all over again so
that he could turn the tables and reject her? It was a
mind-boggling thought. Was he really that devious?

'Rhiannon.' Pasqual's voice broke into her thoughts.
'I think we should have lunch before we dock at Santa
Cruz.'

'I'm not hungry,' she returned flatly. 'If you want
something get it yourself.' Why should she be his slave
as well as his prisoner?

She had expected an argument, even looked forward to it, and she was amazed when he cut the engine
and dropped anchor. But her amazement turned to
anger when, as time lengthened, she realised he was
taking her at her word and eating lunch by himself.

She crossed the deck and peered down into the galley. The appetising smell of vegetable soup wafted her
way, making her realise how hungry she was.

'There's plenty left if you want some.'

She shrank back, not realising he was aware of her
presence. 'No, thanks.'

'You'll be sorry later,' he said warningly. 'I have no
intention of stopping for you.'

'Don't worry, you won't have to.' She descended and
faced him in the dining area. 'As far as I'm concerned
we don't even need to go ashore. I can't see what pleasure either of us will get out of it.' And then, as the
appalling alternative struck her, 'On the other hand,
I've never actually been up Mount Teide. Perhaps we
could go there?'

His mouth twisted sardonically. As always he knew
exactly what thoughts were running through her mind.
'Whatever you wish. Are you going to be sensible and
eat?'

Rhiannon looked at his half-empty soup bowl and
decided this was no time to be a martyr. If they were

going to climb Mount Teide she would need all her energy. She nodded resignedly. 'I think I will have some.'

'Good. There's a saucepan on the stove. Help yourself,' and he continued to spoon up the remains of his soup.

When they had finished he left her to tidy the galley, and soon they were nosing into the port of Santa Cruz.

The roar of cars and the clamour of voices speaking a dozen different languages was welcome to Rhiannon. It was like a breath of fresh air to see and hear all these other people around them. She had had enough of Pasqual's company and didn't know for how much longer she could put up with it.

He hired a car and soon they were speeding out of the bustling capital, and she tried to ignore the fact that they were thrust closer together here than on the boat. The landscape was lush and green, with mile after mile of banana plantations and tomato fields, hillsides dense with eucalyptus and pines. 'Did you know,' asked Pasqual, 'that the pine absorbs moisture from the clouds and transmits it through its roots to the earth?'

Rhiannon didn't, and shook her head, too busy looking about her to want to indulge in conversation. Each island in the Canaries was different, and she wanted to miss nothing. Marion had been too busy chattering on their coach tour for her to take in very much of the scenery.

The roadside was fragrant with honeysuckle and mimosa, colourful with poinsettia and jacaranda, and gardens were stunning with delicate frangipani trees and beds of Bird-of-Paradise flowers.

As the road gained altitude there was a corresponding drop in temperature, and the higher they climbed the more spectacular were the views. The colours below darkened until the greens of the valley faded into grey, and Pasqual told her that they were actually within the perimeter of Mount Teide.

The volcano on Cerrillo was nothing compared to this, one of the earth's largest volcanic craters. The only sign of life now was scrub, the road cutting through hills of stratified lava in black and white, red and grey.

They finally stopped and took the cable-car, pitching and tossing for the eight-minute journey over snow-covered slopes, Rhiannon both excited and scared, clinging unconsciously to Pasqual's arm. And still they were faced with a short hike to the summit.

'Are you game?' asked Pasqual.

The air was so thin here that Rhiannon wondered whether she would manage it, but she nodded nevertheless and they trudged solidly upwards, and she was glad she had made the effort.

The view was spectacular—all of the Canary Islands visible on this clear day. Rhiannon was delighted when she found a shrinking blue violet tucked beneath a rock—the only flower ever to grow on Mount Teide.

She inhaled the clean pure air and turned with a smile to Pasqual. It felt good to be alive, and she was suddenly glad he had brought her.

'Look, there's Cerrillo,' he said.

She could see nothing.

He placed his arm about her shoulders and she could smell his husky aftershave and feel the warmth of his body despite the coolness of the air, and she wanted to snatch away but dared not. He bent his head towards her and pointed a finger so that their eyes were both trained in the same direction. 'There, Rhiannon, that tiny dot directly in front of you, to the right of that larger one.'

She held her breath, trying to stop herself from trembling. How foolishly she was behaving! She found the island and looked in tight-lipped silence. It was impossible to make out any detail; it was just a blob in the ocean. And yet she fed her eyes on it greedily. Soon, very soon, Cerrillo would be nothing more than a memory. What had been a dream for her parents, and a happy home for herself, had been torn from them by this man's grasping fingers. She must remember that. She must never let herself be swayed by his powerful personality.

'Do you see it?' He turned to look at her and frowned. 'What's wrong?'

'I was thinking of my father—and you—and the fact that Yurena would still be ours if you hadn't been so obsessed with buying it.' Her voice was sharp and hostile, her whole body rejecting him.

'Tony didn't have to sell,' he rasped, his eyes abruptly angry. 'The decision was his. I didn't force him.'

'But you made your offer too generous to refuse. You were charming and smooth, and even I couldn't convince him that he was making a mistake.'

'And it still bothers you that you weren't able to have your own way?' There was tolerant amusement on his face now. 'When are you going to grow up, Rhiannon, and realise that we all have to give in graciously at some time in our lives?'

'Maybe I was selfish,' she cried, 'but don't you think the way you went about it had a lot to do with it?'

He shook his head. 'You admitted that even if I'd been honest right from the start you still wouldn't have agreed to the take-over. I think it's your pride that's hurt more than anything else. You won't admit that you could have been wrong. I found Tony more than willing to sell. He was worried about your reaction, naturally, but he's only stayed on all these years because of you. He wanted out as soon as your mother

died. It would only have been a matter of time before
the inevitable happened.'

Rhiannon remained silent. Was he right? Had her
father given up finding happiness back home in
England just so that she could do what she wanted?
Was she as spoilt as Pasqual seemed to think, always
used to getting her own way?

Well, she was certainly not getting her own way now.
Pasqual was making sure of that. How long would he
keep her? How long before this emotion-ridden
journey ended?

Perhaps if she changed her attitude and pretended
to be actually enjoying it, he might take her back home.
It was worth a try.

CHAPTER SEVEN

RHIANNON expected Pasqual to drive back to his cruiser, but instead he headed west and finally drew up in front of a hotel proudly wearing the PLG crest.

During the journey she had remained silent, too engrossed in her thoughts to ask where they were going, unconscious even of the quizzical looks that he threw her. Now she glanced about her with a frown. Was he combining business with pleasure? Or were they simply stopping here for something to eat?

Following as he strode inside, Rhiannon was amused to observe the staff jump to attention. He walked across to the reception desk and she looked about her. It was a typical PLG hotel—much bigger than Yurena, busier too, and more lively, thronging with young people. She shuddered to think this might happen to her former home.

It was the type of establishment her parents had abhorred, and what had made them develop a hotel that was completely different. And although a lot of the people here were the same age as herself, Rhiannon felt quite alienated. No doubt because she had been brought up in a contrasting environment, had grown used to it, and now actually preferred it.

When Pasqual rejoined her he led the way towards the lift. Rhiannon frowned and stopped, having already spotted the dining room on the ground floor. 'Where are we going?' she asked suspiciously.

Pasqual's brows rose, as though it should have been obvious. 'To my suite.'

'We're staying here? Why?' Rhiannon's heart beat uncomfortably fast. Now what was he up too? Did he think she would react differently with a change of surroundings?

'So that we can continue our sightseeing from here tomorrow,' he answered reasonably. 'Unless you've seen enough of Tenerife?'

She shrugged. 'It's your holiday.'

'Yours too,' he reminded her. 'You're forgetting this whole trip is for your benefit. I want you to enjoy yourself.' His smile suggested that he was having no difficulty himself.

'When I'm your prisoner? How can I?' She glared into the open mockery of his eyes, her resolution to put on an act completely forgotten.

'I'm quite sure,' he said calmly, 'that if you relax and think more about the past you'll find me excellent company.'

She tossed her head. 'That's impossible. You're an arrogant, self-opinionated swine, and I'll never forgive you for this as long as I live! The longer you keep me your prisoner the more I shall hate you!'

'Poor Rhiannon.' His lips curled in amusement. 'What a terrible time you're having! Why don't you climb down? You might surprise yourself. We had a good relationship—I see no reason why we can't get back on that same footing.'

'There's every reason in the world,' she snapped, 'and don't you think we ought to move?' They had attracted a lot of attention, staff and guests alike listening openly to their conversation.

He looked around, only just noticing their audience, and with a mock bow in their direction, he took her elbow and guided her into the waiting lift.

'I suppose you think you're very clever,' she shot coldly. 'What are we going to do for clothes? All we've got is what we stand up in.'

'There are shops right here in the hotel,' he informed her cheerfully. 'You don't have to worry about a thing.'

Rhiannon fumed as they were whisked silently and swiftly upwards. She saw no point in arguing. Pasqual always got his own way—exactly what he had accused her of doing! But that, she supposed, was different.

When the lift stopped she followed him along a short corridor, stopping abruptly when Pasqual pushed open a door.

He turned and smiled encouragingly. 'Don't stand there. Come in.'

'I'm not sleeping with you!'

His smile widened. 'I didn't dream for one moment that you'd allow it. You're forgetting how well I know you, Rhiannon. There are two bedrooms, you'll be quite safe.'

Like she would in a cage full of vipers! With more than a hint of unease she moved inside, observing the rich reds and golds, modern Spanish blending with traditional. It was luxurious without being vulgar, but a waste, if it sat here unused most of the time—and she didn't trust him one inch. Or was it herself she did not trust?

He opened the door. 'Here you are. This is your room.'

She took a deep breath, and with only a cursory glance said, 'Very nice.'

He still remained annoyingly cheerful. 'Perhaps you'd like to go and select whatever clothes you'll need, then you can freshen up before we eat.'

With her chin high and her eyes bright Rhiannon swung out of the room. It was a relief to get away from him, and she wished she knew what devious thoughts

were going through his mind. Would he ever give her
any peace? she asked herself achingly.

As she went down in the lift she wondered whether
she dared risk running away. But where to—with no
money? Perhaps she could tell someone here what he
was doing to her? But would they believe her story? He
was a big name and eminently respected; they would
think she was making it up.

Resignedly she found her way to the shops, taking
her time choosing. A dress and sandals for this evening, a nightdress and undies, a suntop for tomorrow,
and when she returned Pasqual was nowhere in sight,
although she thought she heard him moving about in
his room.

With relief Rhiannon took a leisurely shower, pondering, as she slipped into her new brown and gold
chiffon dress, what sort of an evening they were going
to have, wishing with all her heart that she had never
set eyes on him. Why hadn't she realised that his sort
were not to be trusted? If she hadn't got entangled with
him in the first place she wouldn't be here now.

Once ready she found him standing looking out of
the sitting room window, smoke from a cigar wrea-
thing above his head. It had grown dark outside, and
their eyes met in his reflection. Pasqual turned and his
warm smile suggested that nothing at all was wrong
between them. 'I like that, it suits you,' he observed.

Rhiannon found his praise pleasing despite her ani-
mosity, and she murmured a quiet, 'Thank you.' All
eyes would be on them in the restaurant, and hard
though it would be she knew it was best they appeared
friends.

And she had to admit that he looked pretty devastating himself in slate-grey slacks and a pale blue shirt,
but deliberately she kept her eyes averted. It annoyed
her that she felt this awareness every time they were

close. What right had he to have this power over her?

'If you're ready, we'll go?'

She nodded. 'I'm ravenous!'

As she had anticipated they attracted a lot of attention and pretending there was nothing wrong was one of the most difficult things she had ever had to do.

But all thoughts fled her mind as she ate. The food was excellent, especially the chicken served with a sauce of chilli peppers, spice and chocolate. It was the very best she had tasted. She had thought their own cook good, but this one was even better, and she was lavish in her praise.

'I always insist on a high standard,' said Pasqual, looking pleased. 'But the cook at Yurena is good too. I shall not change him.'

Would Carlos be grateful for that? she wondered. If there were changes, too many changes, he would not be happy. He liked the atmosphere at Yurena. He had a large family and lived on Cerrillo, and if he was forced to find work elsewhere it would affect them all.

During the meal she managed to relax, but when Pasqual suggested a walk to finish off the evening she hastily declined. 'Not for me, thank you. It's been a tiring day.' And she had had as much of his company as she could tolerate!'

'In that case, I'll go myself,' he said, stroking her cheek with the back of his fingers, then trailing them down her throat and over her shoulder.

'*Buenas noches*, Rhiannon.' He leaned forward and kissed her, a light impersonal kiss that meant nothing and yet everything. It was as though he was telling her what would happen once he did come to bed.

'*Buenas noches*,' she whispered, her cheeks suddenly flaming. Ignoring the lift, she ran up the stairs and once in the privacy of her room threw herself down on the bed.

Damn Pasqual! How dared he behave in this manner! She was a fool for responding to his intense masculinity, she knew that, but it was not something easily ignored. Even at the height of her anger she still felt the pull of his magnetism, and even when she reminded herself that he had been stringing her along her body remained traitorously responsive.

She dragged off her dress and slid betweeen the sheets, and it seemed like hours before she finally heard Pasqual return. She held her breath, expecting him to come in, and when he went straight to his room she did not know whether to be disappointed or relieved.

Her awareness of him was increasing by the minute—which was probably what he intended. But had he realised exactly how tortuous she would find it? She wanted him more and more, her whole body aching with longing and desire until she thought it would drive her insane.

She slept little that night, tossing and turning, vitally conscious of Pasqual next door. Was he sleeping? Was his conscience bothering him? She guessed not.

When morning came her head was pounding, and she felt cross and irritable and decided she'd had as much as she could take. She bounced out of bed and out of her room, and banged on Pasqual's door.

'Come in,' he called, and when she went inside he was sitting up, looking disgustingly fresh and cheerful.

His tanned muscular chest was bare, and she guessed the rest of him was as well. The colour in her cheeks deepened and the breath seemed suddenly driven out of her body and she asked herself what she was doing here. But it was too late to turn back.

'To what do I owe this pleasure?' he enquired, his eyes registering her nakedness beneath the sheer nightdress, making her wish she had stopped to pull on some clothes.

'It's not what you think,' she shot hastily, seeing the speculative gleam in his eyes. 'Nothing like that at all.'

'No?' Cynical brows rose. 'That's a pity. I've lain awake most of the night imagining you in my bed. I thought for a moment my prayers had been answered.'

'I won't pretend to be sorry that I've disappointed you,' she scoffed. He did not look as though he'd lost any sleep. Not like herself. She hadn't looked in the mirror but could imagine her pasty complexion and the shadows beneath her eyes.

'I want you to take me back to Cerrillo!' she demanded shrilly.

His brows rose. 'Now?'

'Yes, now!' she cried.

'And what's brought about this sudden decision?'

'I can't take any more,' she said, her voice suddenly quiet.

'You must know what my answer will be.'

'But why?' she demanded. 'Why are you keeping me prisoner?'

His brows rose. 'Isn't it obvious? I intend to resurrect what we once had going for us—without the disturbing influence of Miguel.'

'To what end?' she demanded, 'so that you can drop me flat when you've finished with me? I have no intention of becoming one of your exes. You preach about Miguel, but what's happened to the girl I saw you with? I'm amazed you've not popped out to see her while we're here. Or did you see her last night? You were gone a long time. Is that why you're looking so pleased with yourself this morning?'

He grinned. 'You sound jealous, my darling.'

Rhiannon tossed her head scornfully. 'You can do what you like, so long as you take me back. This is ridiculous! If you're going to wait for me to change my mind you'll be wandering the ocean for ever.'

'Which doesn't sound a bad idea,' he admitted pleasantly. 'What's it like, Rhiannon, not getting your own way?'

She could cheerfully have thrown something at him. Instead she took a deep breath and counted silently to ten, turning briefly to look out of the window. Hearing him move, she glanced across—and then wished she hadn't when he threw back the sheets and leapt out of bed.

There was no describing the feelings aroused in her by the sight of his magnificent naked body. Fire streaked through her loins and she averted her eyes quickly. If her legs had not felt so leaden she would have made a dash for the door. Instead she remained rooted to the spot, hardly able to breathe when he halted only centimetres away from her.

His hands touched her shoulders. 'Why not admit, Rhiannon, that the real reason you're here is because you want me? It's coming across in waves so strong I'd have to be blind not to see it.'

She refused to look at him, glancing instead at some point in the middle of his chest. But when his fingers lifted her chin she could not hide the longing that filled every vein and every nerve. Her heart pounded unforgivably and she grew conscious of a tell-tale pulse in the base of her throat.

He lowered his head and his mouth touched the flickering pulse. His hands slid to her back and then her waist, urging her over-heated body against his.

'No, Pasqual, this isn't what I want.' She made a feeble effort to push him away, but all the strength seemed to have drained out of her and instead she found herself clinging to him.

'Yes, you do, we both want it.' His tone grew deeper and his mouth found hers, and Rhiannon could not fight. She wondered whether Pasqual was right and this had been at the back of her mind when she came to his room. She could have waited until breakfast to tackle him. Why hadn't she?

Her lips parted and her hands snaked convulsively around his broad back. He had destroyed her love, but even so the raw need was still there—and the minutes lengthened.

When they were compelled to draw apart for breath she was shocked by the ravaged lines on his face. He groaned and with fingers that trembled tore her nightdress from neck to hem, giving a cry of satisfaction when he pulled her naked body against his.

Rhiannon could not deny that it felt good for her too, even though she knew it was pure need that drove him on. They were both satisfying a carnal desire. He was a highly sexual man, and being forced into his company for hours upon end it should have been obvious where they would finish up.

He lifted her and carried her to the bed, his hungry kisses smothering her face, his hand covering a breast, urging it to burgeoning fullness, her nipple teased and tormented until she felt as though she were dying, so exquisite was his torture. When his mouth replaced his hand and he sucked her throbbing nipple into the hotness of his mouth she could not contain a moan of pure pleasure.

He lifted glazed eyes to look at her, and she took his head between her hands and leaned forward to kiss him. His lips were hungry and tasted of herself, and she wanted to cry out that it was wrong but she couldn't.

Her breathing was deep and erratic, and she lay back again, her hips gyrating of their own volition, his hand moving over the flatness of her stomach and hips— causing fresh agonies of desire to race through her.

Rhiannon was not sure how much of this she could take. He was sending her mindless, making her forget everything except the pleasure of his lovemaking. 'Pasqual,' she whispered unconsciously, her fingers threading despairingly through his hair. 'Love me, Pasqual, love me!'

He stilled a moment. 'You'll never know how much I've wanted you to say that.'

It was the sound of his voice that penetrated her consciousness, made her realise exactly what she had said, and her eyes widened in horror. 'No, no, it's not what I want. What am I saying? What are you doing to me? Get away, Pasqual, get away!'

His brows beetled into a frown, his eyes glazed with passion and desire. 'Damn you, Rhiannon! This is no time to back out.'

'I should have stopped you earlier. I don't know why I didn't.' She struggled to roll from beneath him. 'Let me go, Pasqual, let me get up!'

'I promise you, I'll make a much better lover than Miguel.'

'Miguel has nothing to do with this,' she sobbed.

'Then what's wrong?'

'This is wrong. I refuse to be one of your women, Pasqual.'

'One of my women?' His eyes were half-hooded, making it difficult now to read their expression. 'You're jealous of all the other girls I've made love to?'

Jealous as hell, but she wouldn't tell him. 'Jealousy has nothing to do with it. But I have my pride, Pasqual. I couldn't live with myself if I let you make love to me now.'

'It would be such an ordeal?' he mocked, heaving himself up, hiding admirably the frustration he must be feeling.

Rhiannon rolled off the bed, snatching one of the sheets to wrap round her, wishing he would put something on too. It was not easy looking at him when he was so obviously still hungering for love.

'It wouldn't work,' she said quietly.

'Then the next time,' he said with a confident smile, 'I shall just have to make sure that it does.'

'There won't be a next time,' she snapped.

'No?' His brows slid up. 'I wouldn't be too sure of that, Rhiannon. You've proved very positively that you're not immune. I'm willing to lay a bet that before the end of our holiday you'll be only too anxious to share my bed.'

Rhiannon yanked open the door, turning to contemptuously flash the emerald-green of her eyes. 'It's odd, I never thought you were the type of man to back a loser.'

CHAPTER EIGHT

BREAKFAST was served in Pasqual's suite, but Rhiannon couldn't eat. The mere thought of food choked her, and sitting opposite him, she squirmed in her seat. She had made such a fool of herself. She had been so weak, so stupid. What on earth had possessed her? She had entered his room with the intention of forcing him to take her home—and ended up in his bed begging him to make love to her. Would she ever be able to forget her humiliation?

'You're not hungry?' he remarked, spreading jam lavishly on his roll and biting into it with even white teeth.

She shook her head, but when he grinned, only too well aware of what was wrong, she said viciously, 'Perhaps I ought to go on hunger strike? Perhaps then you'd realise you're fighting a losing battle. I bet if my father knew how you were treating me he'd wish he'd never conspired with you. Wait till he finds out!'

'And exactly how am I treating you?' His blue eyes glinted humorously. 'Have I hurt you? Have I degraded you? Have I forced you to do anything against your will?'

She hung her head. It had been a foolish remark. 'You're making me respond to you against my will.'

'And is that so bad?'

'Yes, it is!' she cried. 'I don't want to love you, Pasqual. I want to hate you—I do hate you. You're the most insufferable man I've ever met!'

He buttered another roll, smiling to himself, and she wondered if anything ever upset him.

Rhiannon scraped her chair back and got up.

'Now where are you going?'

Blue eyes met green and for several hostile seconds she managed to hold his gaze. Then she shrugged. 'To pack. We're leaving, aren't we?'

'When you've eaten breakfast,' he replied steadily. 'Sit down, Rhiannon, stop acting like a spoilt child.'

With bad grace she dropped back into her seat, picked up a croissant and bit into it savagely.

He watched until she had eaten every last flake and drained her coffee cup, and only then did he relent and smile. 'Good, now we can go. I'm sure you must feel better?'

Rhiannon chose not to answer, marching stiffly into her room and slamming the door, wishing she could see the end to this ordeal.

They left the hotel and visited the Botanical Garden just outside Puerto de la Cruz—a cool green tropical sanctuary that temporarily soothed Rhiannon's troubled mind.

Pasqual pointed out a tree-house in the intertwined roots and branches of a South American fig tree. There was cactus corner and a tiny zoo, and birds of all sorts flew in from outside to enjoy the scenery.

But she could summon up no real enthusiasm, despite Pasqual's continued cheerfulness. The drive back to Santa Cruz was long and tiring, and she was glad when the day ended and they were back on his cruiser.

In bed that night she recalled the feel of his hands and his mouth on her skin, and awoke again feelings she had tried hard all day to suppress. It was all very well telling him that she hated him and that she didn't want him touching her. Her body did say differently, as he had correctly pointed out. She tossed and turned, and at length could lie there no longer. She needed a drink, something strong, something to knock her out and make her forget these idiotic yearnings.

Pasqual kept the spirits in a cabinet in the lounge, and the key was always in the lock. It was pitch black, and she groped her way blindly across the room, reluctant to switch on the light for fear of alerting him.

She found the gin bottle and taking it over to the table carefully poured out what she thought was half a glass, but when she lifted it to her lips the liquid spilled over. With a muffled curse she returned the glass to the table, misjudged her aim and sent the bottle flying.

The noise was deafening, and she waited with bated breath for Pasqual to appear, blinking owlishly when he snapped on the light.

He took in the scene with one swift sweep of the room, his mouth twisting derisively. 'A secret gin drinker, I see?'

He had on the cotton slacks he had worn yesterday, but his chest was bare and his hair tousled, and he looked no less sexy for having been disturbed out of his sleep.

'I couldn't sleep,' she defended hotly.

'So I gathered. But did you have to creep around like an intruder? How much have you drunk?' He looked at her empty glass, picking up the bottle which was also almost empty.

'None,' she snapped. 'I haven't had a chance.'

'Then I suggest a cup of hot milk will do you more good.' He replaced the bottle in the cabinet, and removed her glass. Then he mopped up the gin and put some milk on to heat, whistling cheerfully to himself as he worked.

Rhiannon was intensely irritated by his attitude, but nevertheless could not take her eyes off him. She admired the display of muscles across his back and chest, and found something appealing in the unkempt appearance of his hair and naked feet.

He was apparently unconscious of her gaze, and her hungry eyes followed his every move. Had he guessed that he was the reason she could not sleep? Did he know that she regretted putting a stop to his love making? That she longed for him more with each hour that passed, despite knowing that she could be no more than a passing affair? It was becoming increasingly difficult to dismiss him from her mind—and she did not know how she was going to get through the rest of the holiday without giving in.

He placed her mug and a plate of biscuits in front of her and sat opposite, cradling his own beaker between his hands, his eyes boring into hers. 'How about telling me why you can't sleep?'

She shrugged. Had he really not guessed? 'I don't know why.'

'Usually,' he said slowly, 'it's because a person's mind is too active. What were you thinking about?' He watched her intently over the edge of his mug as he took a sip.

He did know! He was playing games with her. 'I prefer not to say,' she answered quietly.

'Then suppose I tell you? You wish you hadn't stopped me last night?'

Rhiannon opened her mouth to protest, then realised he was teasing her. What would he say, she wondered, if she told him it was true? She had never before wanted a man with the same degree of hunger. It was a totally new experience, and all the more humiliating because of the type of man he was. She was not the sort who could indulge in casual affairs. With her it had to be an all or nothing relationship.

But she was beginning to realise that this was one man who would not let her have her own way. She could fight him all she liked and he would not take her home until she was ready, and surprisingly she admired him for it.

'My only regret,' she said slowly, 'was being infatuated by you in the first place.' If she hadn't made such a complete idiot of herself none of this would have happened.

'So—it wasn't love, it was infatuation?' An eyebrow quirked disbelievingly. 'Since when have you arrived at that conclusion?'

She shrugged. 'I've always known.'

'And your feelings for Miguel? Do you love him— or is that infatuation as well?' There was a sudden crispness to his tone. 'I don't think, Rhiannon, that you know what you do feel.'

'And I don't think that you have any right to question me,' she countered. 'You're far from perfect yourself. Although it seems that I'm supposed to accept your girl-friends without question. I'm the one who has to account for daring to be friendly with another man.'

'Once this holiday's over you're free to go out with Miguel, or whomever you like,' he announced carelessly.

Her eyes widened. 'How generous!' He was simply saying that because he knew he was doing his best to make sure she didn't want another man. And how well he was succeeding! Even at this point her whole body was responding, aided by the fact that they were both near-naked. Her silk nightdress with its lace inserts left little to the imagination. It had been terrifyingly expensive for what there was of it, but Pasqual had insisted and since he was footing the bill she had not argued. Now she wished she wore something more practical. She felt defenceless, both her body and mind revealed.

'But until then, you're stuck with me.'

He looked so pleased about the situation that Rhiannon wanted to hit him. More and more these days she felt the need for a physical battle. He was so relentless in his pursuit of her that sometimes she wondered whether it wouldn't be as well to give in.

She looked at his chest, at its scattering of light brown hairs, at the steady rise and fall. At his hands holding the mug, strong brown fingers, square at the end and well manicured. At the taut column of his throat, his firm chin and wide mouth. His nose, straight and slightly flared, his ears, well-shaped and close to his head. She looked anywhere except into his eyes—because she was afraid.

A girl could drown in the haunting depths of his eyes. They had the power to turn bones to jelly and blood to water. He was a dangerous, exciting, and extremely sensual male—and if he truly loved her, instead of merely desiring her, she would have been the happiest girl alive.

'Have you nothing to say?'

The taunting words made her look at him sharply. 'What's the point? I found out when I asked you to take me home that you always have your own way.'

'And because you can't have yours you thought you'd resort to drink, is that it?'

'It would have helped me sleep,' she declared recklessly.

'Oh, I can think of something much better than gin, or milk,' he said with a confident smile, his hands touching hers across the table.

Although Rhiannon desperately wanted to snatch free she remained still. Let him think she was unaffected. 'You can?' she asked, even though she knew full well what he meant.

'Come to bed with me and I can guarantee that—afterwards—you'll sleep as peaceful as a baby.'

Rhiannon's heart thumped uncomfortably as her eyes met his. His suggestion was tempting. Her body needed him, ached for him, and yet at the same time repudiated him. He was a philanderer. Giving herself to him would be like signing her own death warrant. There would be no life for her afterwards. She would never be able to forgive herself for indulging in a casual affair.

'And put myself in the same category as all the other girls you've bedded?' she demanded brittly.

'You seem so sure that there have been other girls?'

'You never explained about the girl in Tenerife, so what other conclusion can I draw? A man of your age and virility doesn't remain celibate, I'll agree, but that doesn't mean to say I have to be as willing as everyone else.'

His smile was as confident as ever. 'This girl bothers you, does she?' But when she would have withdrawn her hands his grip tightened.

'What do you think?' she demanded. 'Even if your intentions towards me weren't serious, you could at least have kept to one at a time!'

'How green your eyes are,' he mocked, his thumb stroking her fingers. It shot sparks of excitement through her, and once again Rhiannon endeavoured to pull free.

To her surprise he let her go, seeming well pleased at the way the conversation had gone. She tucked her hands on her lap beneath the table, fingers locked, palms sweaty. What a mistake it had been to leave her cabin. Far better to have lain awake the whole night than suffer his taunts.

'I expect your milk's cold,' said Pasqual, his voice normal, all emotional undertones gone. 'I'll reheat it.'

Rhiannon was glad of the brief respite, though she suspected all the time in the world would not be enough. She needed to be free of Pasqual before she got any peace of mind. And yet even fleeing as far away as England might not be enough. In mind he would be with her always.

When he returned and placed the mug in front of her Rhiannon desperately sipped the scalding milk, ignoring the fact that it was burning her throat, anxious only to seek the privacy of her cabin.

He watched her closely. 'How are you feeling now? Do you think you'll sleep?'

'Like a log,' lied Rhiannon. 'I apologise once again for disturbing you. I'll try not to do it again.' In fact she would make a point of never doing it. She felt less like sleep now than she had in the first place.

But, comforted by the milk, she found her limbs soon grew heavy and she slept, hearing no more until the movement of the ship and the hum of its engine told her they were on the move.

Peering through her cabin window, Rhiannon could see nothing but shiny blue ocean. Where were they heading this time? she asked herself resignedly. Not back to Cerrillo, that was for sure. Pasqual was determined to bend her to his will before heading home. It was a pity circumstances were such as they were, because it could have been an unforgettable cruise.

It did not take her long to shower and dress. There was a pot of coffee keeping hot in the galley and she poured herself a cup and took it up on deck.

Pasqual was at the wheel, his eyes narrowed against the sunlight. He looked wide-awake and fresh, white shorts and T-shirt emphasising his tan, the sun gilding his hair where it curled below his peaked cap. As always she found him excitingly, sexily male, unable to deny the physical attraction that she felt.

'*Buenos dias,* Rhiannon. How are you this morning?' His blue eyes rested on her face and she knew that he had no need to ask. He knew her too well. He had the uncanny ability of being able to see right into her mind.

There were shadows beneath her eyes, she knew, which were a dead giveaway, but she lifted her chin fractionally. 'Fully rested, thanks to your milk. What time is it?' It looked as though they had been moving for quite a while. There was no land in sight anywhere, nothing but the blue of the ocean. Not even a seabird. Just herself—and Pasqual—and fate.

'Well after ten. I did contemplate waking you, but decided it wouldn't make me very popular.'

She glanced at him sharply, about to make a quick retort, but saw the gleam in his eye and knew he was goading her. 'Where are we going?' she asked with quiet dignity.

'Gomera. Your type of island—quiet, no airstrip, not many hotels.'

'Yes, I know,' she said. Gomera reminded her a lot of Cerrillo.

'You've been there before?'

Rhiannon shook her head. 'I've only heard about it, but it sounds delightful.'

'It is, I assure you,' he confirmed, 'and I hope you appreciate that I'm doing all I can to please you.'

She glanced at him sharply. 'You know what I want. This whole trip's a ridiculous farce so far as I'm concerned. I don't know what Daddy was thinking of to agree it with you.'

'Tony thinks I'm good for you.'

Her eyes widened.

'He thinks you need a firm hand.'

'At my age? I'm twenty-four. I'm quite capable of making my own decisions and running my own life—if people will let me,' she added caustically.

His lips quirked. 'From what I've seen so far you haven't exactly proved it. You tried to stop your father selling, when it was what he really wanted. You even accused me of trying to use you for that purpose, when it was you alone I was interested in.'

'I did accept your explanation,' interrupted Rhiannon coldly.

'But you weren't capable of making the decision for yourself. You're no judge of mankind, Rhiannon. Involving yourself with Miguel proves that. He's not——'

'Let's leave Miguel out of this,' she snapped.

'Is it pining for your lover that makes you so irritable?' Pasqual enquired silkily. 'Is that why you can't bear me to touch you—because you're always thinking of him?'

'At least he would never force me into anything against my will!'

His brows rose. 'If you stopped playing the offended innocent you might surprise yourself and find out that you enjoy my company after all.'

'Like I'd enjoy being confronted by a wounded tiger!' she thrust, turning her back on him. The trouble was she had to be on her guard for her own peace of mind. It would be so easy to drift into a relationship. Despite the fact that she knew him for what he was it was still impossible to ignore the strong chemical reaction he set up in her.

She went below and washed her cup and emptied the coffee pot. It was tempting to stay down away from him, but that was probably what he expected; so with her head held high and a towel and her suncream clutched in her hand she went back up and lay down on the deck.

It was not long before he set the ship on automatic rudder and joined her. Although Rhiannon did not open her eyes she was very conscious of him, and almost got up and walked away. Why was he being so persistent when she had made it perfectly clear that she wanted nothing to do with him?

They lay without speaking for several minutes, and then Rhiannon felt his fingers on her cheek, stroking lightly, tracing the outline of her cheekbones, the shape of her chin, the contours of her lips.

With an effort she kept still, but eventually she felt compelled to glance at him. There was a look of raw hunger on his face which both scared and excited her. Although his eyes were instantly guarded he did not stop what he was doing. His hand slid along her throat, cupping her chin, holding it firmly so that she could not move. But when his mouth sought hers, erotic and sensual, she turned her head deliberately away.

It would be so easy to submit and accept what he was offering, but if she wanted any self-respect left then she must never again respond.

'Rhiannon?'

'I'm not a sex object,' she thrust savagely, 'so don't treat me as one!'

'But you're not immune to me. Dammit, Rhiannon, I've had enough of your silly games!' He rolled on top of her, his mouth bruising, one hand on her breast, the top of her bikini torn away in his urgency.

Her heart thumped and her whole body cried out for fulfilment. But the sane part of her mind knew that she would regret later any abandoning of her morals, and somehow she managed to lie limp and lifeless, ignoring the sweet torture of his hands and mouth.

It took him a long time to accept that he was getting nowhere, and for the first time on this cruise his self-control deserted him. With a savage cry he pushed himself up, his face flushed and angry.

'And how much did that cost you?' he whipped. 'Don't think I'm not aware of your feelings. If I'd persevered I could have had you, and you know it. But that isn't the way I want things. I'll bide my time. I shall get what I want in the end, have no fear about that.'

Rhiannon waited until he had gone below before sitting up and pulling her cotton wrap about her shoulders. Thank goodness he did not know how close to submission she had been! There was still a hunger inside her and she wrapped her arms about herself, rocking backwards and forwards until at length she grew calmer and lay down again, and was finally lulled to sleep by the gentle movement of the boat.

When she awoke she had a headache, and pushing herself up, she made her way to her cabin, passing Pasqual at the wheel. He had completely recovered his good humour and he tossed her a smile, looking as if he was actually enjoying the challenge of making her yield. Why, oh, why, she asked herself for the hundredth time, wouldn't he accept that she would never change her mind? He could batter away at her defences for ever, it would make no difference. She could be as determined as he.

By the time she reached her cabin her head was thumping. She reached for her bag beneath the bed to take a couple of aspirin, and almost fell when an attack of dizziness spun her off balance.

She went through to the galley and filled a glass with water, swallowing down the tablets and then returning to her cabin to lie on the bed. What was wrong with her? She was beginning to feel quite ill.

For several minutes she lay there, the room spinning about her head so fast that it was nothing but a blur. Was it because she hadn't eaten any breakfast? She did feel slightly nauseous. Or was it perhaps seasickness? But no, she would have experienced that before now.

She felt hot, though strangely she wasn't sweating, but she did feel acutely sick and was compelled to dash through to the bathroom. Then suddenly everything went black.

'Rhiannon! Rhiannon! Can you hear me? Rhiannon! Speak to me!'

Her vision cleared and she looked up at the male form leaning over her. 'Where am I? Who are you?' What was she doing on the floor?

'*Mal de cir!* You stupid girl!'

A pair of strong arms swept her up and she was carried through to a tiny room and dumped on a bed. But why wouldn't everything keep still? 'What's happened? What's wrong with me?' she muttered.

Still no satisfactory answer. And whoever the man was he looked angry. He disappeared, and when he came back he pushed a thermometer into her mouth and pressed his fingers lightly over the pulse in her wrist. Was he a doctor?

'What are you doing?' She struggled, but it was an effort. Everything was an effort. And her head felt like it was about to explode. 'I want to be sick,' she said. 'Let me get up.'

'I don't think you'll make it.' His lips were grim as he ripped off her clothes, and the next second she was swung up again into his arms and carried through to a bathroom where the tub was already filling with cold water.

Half-conscious as she was, Rhiannon tried to fight when she realised he was going to drop her in.

'Listen to me, Rhiannon!' he barked. 'You've got sunstroke. I must act quickly. What the hell did you lie in the sun so long for?—and without your hat. You've lived here long enough to know how strong this North African sun is.'

'Here? Where is here?' The water was cold, icy cold, and she was hot, burning up. What did the man say? Sunstroke? What was sunstroke?

'We're in the Canary Islands,' came the impatient reply.

'We're on an island? Why is it moving?' She smiled foolishly. 'The island's moving.'

Pasqual let out an angry breath. 'You're on my boat, Rhiannon. Now shut up and let me get on with it!'

His hands furiously massaged her body, rubbing her all over, not missing one inch. She tried to fight him off. She did not know why, but something deep down inside told her that this man was not to be trusted.

But he was strong and he did not let up even when she flailed her arms in every direction. 'Why am I with you? Who are you?'

He grimaced. 'My name's Pasqual. You're on holiday with me.'

'And I'm—Rhiannon, did you say?'

He nodded.

'Where do I live? Are you my friend?'

'Cerrillo. And yes, I'm your friend, a very good friend. So stop fighting, you have nothing to fear.'

'I want to get out. I don't want to sit in here!' Her voice rose to a wail and she struggled to stand. 'I don't think you're my friend. I think you're mad! You're trying to drown me!'

'You can get out all in good time,' he replied patiently. 'I have to bring your temperature down first. It shouldn't take long.'

He continued to massage and Rhiannon continued to verbally abuse him and rise up out of the water. He ignored her outbursts, constantly taking her temperature until at last he announced himself satisfied.

Hauling her up, he wrapped her in a towel and carried her back to the cabin, where he dumped her on the bed. He threw a single sheet over her and stood watching.

Rhiannon screwed up her face as she tried to recall the events leading up to her sunstroke. 'I can't remember. Did I really lie in the sun so long?'

He nodded. 'Really.'

'Why? Am I always that silly?'

'Lately you've been very silly,' he said.

Rhiannon shook her head. 'I feel very confused. You say we're friends, but I don't feel anything for you. And I'm cold. Why did you put me in that water.'

He cursed and took her temperature again, and then began once more to massage her limbs.

'What are you doing? Get your hands off me!'

'Your temperature's still dropping and I'm trying to prevent your blood vessels from constricting. Keep still, damn you!'

He rubbed her until she was glowing and warm and then covered her up with blankets and sat beside the bed.

She closed her eyes, and all was silent save for their breathing.

'How are you feeling now?'

His voice was gruff and concerned, and Rhiannon opened her eyes.

'Better, I think.'

Again he took her temperature and this time he nodded. 'I think the danger's over. You're very lucky— serious sunstroke can be fatal. Are you warm?'

'Yes, thank you,' she whispered.

'Then I suggest you try to get some sleep. I'll leave you for a while, but if you need me don't be afraid to call out.'

Warm and comfortable for the first time in—how long? How long had she spent in that icy bath? Rhiannon had no idea. But, warm now, she felt her limbs grow heavy and it was not long before sleep took over.

It was dark when she awoke and Pasqual was sitting beside her, the lamp casting a golden glow on his hair. He smiled. 'At last! I was getting worried.'

'I'm thirsty,' she announced, 'and hungry.'

'That must mean you're feeling better.' He looked pleased. 'What would you like?'

'Anything.'

'Some chicken breast and bread and butter? A glass of milk?'

'Lovely!'

He was back in such a short space of time that she guessed he must have had it ready and waiting, and he sat and watched as she ate, the lamp casting shadows on his face.

When she had finished he took the plate away and then resumed his seat. 'You were very foolish, Rhiannon. You could have been much worse than you are.'

'I fell asleep. I've no idea how long I lay there.'

'Too long,' he said tightly.

'I suppose I should thank my lucky stars that you knew what to do? You appear to have saved me from a painful experience. Thank you, Pasqual.'

He shrugged. 'Think nothing of it. But you're not better yet. You'll have to stay in bed for a few days.'

'But I feel all right,' she protested, horrified at the thought of being at his mercy. She was remembering things she would far rather forget, like him massaging every inch of her body. Admittedly it had been necessary and his actions were entirely clinical, but what had his thoughts been? Her cheeks flamed and she was glad the semi-darkness hid her embarrassment.

'You'll get up when I say you can,' he announced firmly.

Rhiannon pulled a face, but did not argue for the moment. If she felt like getting up she would, regardless of Pasqual's instructions; but when she went to the bathroom later she discovered that she was far weaker than she expected, and realised the wisdom of his advice.

For most of the time the ship was set on automatic rudder and he sat beside her bed. They played cards and did crossword puzzles, they read books and sometimes simply listened to music, and Rhiannon developed a far deeper understanding of the complexities of this man.

He was doctor and nurse, he was lover and friend; he was her tormentor and her enemy, and yet he was her saviour too. There were so many different facets to his character. She had seen him savage and sometimes gentle, cruel yet sometimes caring.

And as she lay in her bed he made her more aware of him than ever before. The look in his eyes, the touch, the word—they were all designed to stimulate her sexual appetite—but done so unobtrusively that she found herself responding to him almost without being aware of it.

It was a momentous decision when she admitted to herself that her love for him had never really died. Despite the way he had treated her she loved him. Despite the fact that he had been seeing another woman at the same time as herself, despite the fact that he didn't love her and was only after revenge, she loved him. How cruel life was!

Within a couple of days she was desperate to get up. He was driving her insane. If he had made a concerted attack on her defences she could have fought him, but when his methods were so subtle what could she do?

Whether the ship went round in continuous circles or whether it criss-crossed the ocean Rhiannon had no idea, but she could stand it no longer. 'Why don't you take me back to Cerrillo?' she asked on the third day. 'It would save you all this trouble.'

'What trouble?' He was almost purring with pleasure. 'I can think of nothing else I'd rather be doing.' His hand was on hers, his thumb gently stroking.

Rhiannon eyed him coolly, fully convinced that he knew exactly the sensations his seemingly innocent action caused. 'Hasn't it occurred to you that I might not enjoy the situation? That I might not want you sitting beside me for hour after hour?'

'I've not heard you raise any objections.' His brows rose, his blue eyes widened. They were asking a question she would not answer. 'But I think perhaps you're ready to get up.' His hand slid along her arm, sending fresh rivers of ecstasy through her, and hooked itself behind her head, pulling her face close.

Rhiannon drew in a deep breath. She was ready for him, wanted him, needed him. He had primed her to fever-pitch—but giving in was what this game was all about. He thought her illness had given him the upper hand, he thought she was his now to do with what he liked. There had been no cross words between them, no fights, no arguments, nothing but a deeply sensual friendship.

'No, Pasqual, no!' Her tone was high, frightened even—which she was—of herself. 'Just because you say I'm better it doesn't mean you can take advantage.'

His eyes were so close, a clear blue with occasional specks of brown. 'I told you once before, Rhiannon, that I never force myself on a woman. But you want me, as much as I want you. For two days now I've felt your response—don't deny it, I know it's true.'

His hand moved to her mouth, touching the softness of her lips, tracing gently the curves of her nose, closing her eyes with feather-light fingertips—and then kissing her when she least expected it, his mouth and tongue creating erotic explosions of sensation that threatened to blow the top off her head.

Rhiannon fought, with all her strength she fought, but Lord how she wanted him. It was like denying herself life itself. Why was he doing this? Why was he punishing her? Surely what she'd done hadn't been so terrible? Didn't he know how much it hurt to withhold herself from him?

With a savage cry Pasqual pushed away, and she was appalled to see the bitter frustration in his eyes. He looked like a man who had been dealt a death sentence. Had he set his hopes on making love to her once she was better? Was this the reason for his remarkable behaviour? Nothing had been too much trouble for him. He had fetched and carried and made sure she never wanted. And it certainly didn't please him that he was getting no reward in return.

His frustration turned to anger and his expression suggested that he could cheerfully have strangled her. Instead he stormed out of her cabin and a few minutes later the ship's engine started. Battle had recommenced.

CHAPTER NINE

THEY reached Gomera mid-afternoon the following day, and their first glimpse was of an island that was barren and desolate. But Rhiannon had heard of its extraordinary fertility, its underground streams and lush valleys and was not dismayed.

'Do you know,' said Pasqual, as they stepped ashore, 'Christopher Columbus left this very port in 1492 when he set off on the voyage during which he discovered America? If you like we can go and see the Church of Our Lady of the Assumption where he took his last Mass before sailing.'

Rhiannon shrugged uninterestedly. 'Whatever you wish.' He had been very distant over the last twenty-four hours and she could not accept that he was being friendly now.

'It is for your benefit,' he thrust, his eyes blue and savage, piercing right through her.

'Then you're wasting your time,' she flung back. 'I'm sick and fed up with the whole thing. Haven't you realised by now that I won't change?'

She turned her head away, chin high, and looked with forced interest about her. There was the *parador*, a government-run hotel, high on the hillside, reputedly an outstanding work of architecture and landscaping. There were the towering crags which dominated the island, none spectacular by Canarian standards, yet impressive all the same, and she was actually very keen to explore, though she would have much preferred to do so on her own.

'You try my temper sorely. Come on,' Pasqual grabbed her arm, 'we'll take a walk to stretch our legs and afterwards have dinner up at the *parador*.'

Rhiannon threw him an angry glance and wrenched free. 'I've had enough of your hands on me! Just keep away, will you?'

His eyes narrowed and grew thoughtful. 'Is that how it's to be?'

Rhiannon nodded, and they looked at each other for several hate-filled seconds before resuming their walk. The silence between them grew unbearable, and when they reached the church made famous by Columbus Rhiannon glanced at its red-tiled roof and sagging door with little interest.

When they finally returned to the ship to change for dinner his hostility hadn't lessened. Why couldn't he see that it was hopeless and take her home? What did he possibly hope to gain by prolonging the time spent together? She wished she had the answer to these questions.

As soon as they were ready Pasqual found a willing islander to drive them up to the *parador*. It was as beautiful as Rhiannon had imagined, and for the first time that day she felt a genuine spark of pleasure.

But it was short-lived. She could not believe her eyes when, a few minutes after they had sat down to sip their sherry, they were approached by the very same girl she had seen Pasqual with in Tenerife.

'Pasqual, what a lovely surprise! What are you doing here?' The raven-haired beauty leaned forward and touched her lips to his brow, her hand possessively on his arm, her dark sloe-shaped eyes feasting themselves hungrily on his face.

She was even more beautiful close up, her long shining black hair brushing Pasqual's cheek. Her white close-fitting dress revealed more than it concealed and she needed little make-up to enhance her natural beauty.

'Ana!' Pasqual looked as pleased to see the girl as she was him. 'Might I ask the same of you? What a coincidence!' He stood up and held her close for a few seconds, before belatedly remembering Rhiannon.

'Rhiannon, this is Ana. Ana, I'd like you to meet Rhiannon Howarth. Rhiannon is looking after my hotel on Cerrillo.'

'*Buenos tardes*, Rhiannon.' Shining brown eyes smiled confidently into hers. '*Como esta usted?*'

'I'm very well, thank you,' replied Rhiannon stiffly, unable to return the friendly smile. Nor did it escape her notice that he had volunteered no information about Ana. What could he have said? A friend of the family? An ex-girl-friend? She would have believed neither.

'You will join us?' asked Pasqual, signalling to the bar attendant to bring another sherry.

'Mm, love to,' smiled Ana, sliding on to the banquette next to Pasqual. Their shoulders touched and she turned towards him eagerly. 'You still haven't told me what you're doing here?'

Rhiannon observed the warmth of his expression and hated him more than ever.

'Giving Rhiannon a well-deserved holiday before the going gets hard,' he replied smoothly. 'I told you about my new hotel?'

'You did,' agreed Ana, 'and I'm dying to see it. I can't believe that you've bought something so different.'

'Rhiannon and her father assured me there's a real call for this type of holiday. I have high hopes, especially as Rhiannon's staying on to run it.'

Ana looked at Rhiannon. 'Why did you sell, if it's so successful?'

'It was my father's, not mine,' she returned tightly. 'Pasqual persuaded him that his offer was too good to turn down.'

Pasqual's eyes flashed a hot blue. 'Your father was keen to return to England, as you well know. The sale took little effort on my part.'

Ana's fine brows rose into a perfect arch. 'You sound as though you were against it, Rhiannon?'

'I was,' she snapped. 'Pasqual doesn't fool me that he'll continue to run it in the same way. Give him a couple of years and it will be like the rest of his group, and Cerrillo will be ruined.'

'Is that so, Pasqual?' Ana ran her hand lovingly down his arm. 'I'm intrigued. How about taking me to see this controversial place?—and I'll give you my opinion, for what it's worth.'

Her smile was sweet, her eyes beguiling, and Pasqual caught and held her hand. 'I see no reason why you shouldn't join us on the homeward journey. I intend going after we've explored here. We've been away long enough. Have you any other plans?'

'None at all,' shrugged the beautiful girl. 'I'm just drifting around. Until I start my new job I'm a free agent.'

Rhiannon watched this open display of affection and felt sick. She was also surprised by Pasqual's revelation that they were going home. Was it an instant decision brought about by Ana's appearance? Perhaps she ought to thank this other girl? Perhaps Ana had done her a favour without realising it? In any case it was apparent that Pasqual was now losing interest in herself—and wasn't she glad!

They sipped their sherry and studied the menu, and an idea began to formulate in Rhiannon's mind. Why not take this opportunity and see if they had any vacancies here? She could not stay on at Yurena—not now. And as this was the only island she knew that was anything like Cerrillo, it was the obvious solution to her problem.

They moved through into the restaurant, and Pasqual and Ana chatted animatedly as they ate, not seeming to notice that Rhiannon only picked at her food. She had felt bad enough about Pasqual and this other girl before, but to be actually forced to sit and watch them together, neither attempting to hide their feelings, was more than she could stomach.

At the end of the meal she slipped away, and it was a simple matter to find the manager. He was a tall, suave individual whom she might not have trusted had she not been so desperate.

But he looked most impressed by her qualifications. 'At the moment I have no vacancies. However, I will most definitely keep you in mind,' he told her smoothly. 'How much notice would you need to give, if anything does crop up?'

'Not a lot,' said Rhiannon. 'I'm under no contract at the moment.' Probably an oversight on Pasqual's part, but one which she would not hesitate to take advantage of.

'Good. I must admit we do have a pretty frequent turnover of staff—probably because the island's so quiet. Most people prefer somewhere more lively. You may be hearing from me sooner than you think.'

Rhiannon smiled and they shook hands, and she went back to her seat feeling pleased. Pasqual and Ana were still talking earnestly but when he invited Ana to join them right now she felt like screaming. This really was taking things too far!

Had he finally accepted that she, Rhiannon, wanted nothing more to do with him? Couldn't he wait to take up where he had left off with this other girl? Ana was welcome to him, but at least he could have waited. He needn't have shown how eager he was to get a bed companion. Because this was inevitably where they would end up.

Her temper was at boiling point as they left the hotel and were driven back down to the harbour. She went straight to her cabin and then leaned against the door trying to listen to what was going on outside.

But all was quiet, though it was not difficult to imagine that they were locked in each other's arms. She undressed and climbed into bed, not even bothering to clean off her make-up, and that night was one of the longest she had ever spent.

The following morning Ana and Pasqual had already eaten when she got up. Not that she felt hungry. Two cups of coffee and a dry roll were all she managed before joining them in the jeep Pasqual had hired.

Ana had already made herself comfortable in the front, but she smiled warmly at Rhiannon. 'I hope you don't mind me sitting here? We'll take it in turns.'

What could she say that wouldn't sound catty? She shrugged. 'You can stay there all day if you like.'

'Oh, no, I couldn't do that,' said Ana quickly.

Pasqual looked speculatively at Rhiannon. 'You look tired. Didn't you sleep well?'

She clenched her teeth. Did he really need an answer? Had she convinced him so completely that he meant nothing at all to her? Wasn't he aware what this girl's presence meant? 'Not very,' she managed at last.

But he did not look worried. Indeed he smiled and turned back in his seat. They wound their way up and out of San Sebastian, the road taking them through a tunnel where they had a superb view at the other end of one of the island's most fertile valleys, lusciously green with banana plantations.

Rising again, they drove to Agulo, perched on the edge of the cliff. They could even see Tenerife in the distance. And all the time Ana and Pasqual passed comments and snippets of information from one to the other, Rhiannon virtually excluded.

Inland again they arrived at Vallehermosa where the famous palm honey was made. 'Liquid is drained from the palm,' explained Pasqual, for once directing his attention solely towards Rhiannon, 'and cooled slowly until it becomes black and thick. It's the volcanic soil in which they grow which gives the honey its spicy tang.' He even purchased a small jar which he handed politely to her.

They continued their journey on a road which was now nothing more than a dirt track, winding crazily around the mountains. Rhiannon pitched and tossed in the back as they bumped over boulders and stones.

She had taken her turn in the front, thanks to Ana's insistence, and it was definitely more comfortable, but the views from the higher back seat were superb and more than compensated for the discomfort. And besides, she had noticed that Pasqual seemed to prefer the other girl's company.

They stopped often, Rhiannon listening in amazement when she heard the *silbo*, the unique whistling language native to the island. She had read about it, but never expected to hear it used, because these days it was almost obsolete.

Ana was also delighted. 'It was developed before the invention of the telephone as a means of communication across the ravines dividing the little villages,' she explained. 'Each word is relayed separately and people can actually recognise who is whistling. Workmen used to whistle instructions and even parents called their children from the fields in this manner. I think it's marvellous.'

'And if we're having a history lesson don't forget to mention the Guanches,' added Pasqual arrogantly.

Rhiannon had heard tales of the fair-haired, blue-eyed Guanches who had inhabited the islands more than two thousand years ago. They were actually little more than cave men who mummified their dead the same as the Egyptians. Every now and then you met someone who was a definite throwback to this age. Instead of the usual black hair of the Spaniards they had fair hair and blue eyes—the same as Pasqual!

It had never occurred to Rhiannon that his fore-bears were Guanches.

He saw the expression in her eyes and laughed drily. 'Yes, they were my ancestors.'

'I never knew,' she said. 'I assumed you had Nordic blood somewhere in you.'

'I'm a true Spaniard and proud of it,' he confirmed.

'I wish I had blonde hair,' protested Ana.

He smiled. 'You're beautiful as you are, haven't I told you enough times?'

Rhiannon swallowed uncomfortably. All day long these little intimacies had passed between them. Couldn't they forget they weren't alone?

'But it's not fair,' protested Ana. 'I want to be different—like you.'

'I think we ought to get going.' With an abrupt change of subject he climbed into the jeep. 'It's your turn in the back, Ana—and no more complaints, or I'll take the next bend so fast that you'll fall out—and I won't stop to pick you up!'

She bobbed her tongue out and laughed, and they set off on the next leg of their journey. Rhiannon reluctantly envied their easy relationship, recalling the early days when she had felt the same rapport. She wondered how long Pasqual had known this other girl.

Whether their love would last, or whether it would go the same way as her own.

At least they didn't embarrass her by kissing and cuddling, but the bond between them was clearly visible.

It was a tiring day, and when Pasqual suggested they stay the night in Vueltas, a village on the opposite coast to San Sebastian, Rhiannon was for once in complete agreement.

They found rooms in a *pension*, and Rhiannon was too tired to worry what Pasqual and Ana were doing, dropping straight to sleep and hearing nothing until he tapped on her door the next morning. 'Ana and I are ready to go,' he called. 'Do we leave you here, or——'

'I'm coming,' she said, wide awake at once.

But when she went downstairs he and Ana were eating their breakfast, and Ana looked as though she was having difficulty in keeping her eyes open.

'He's a rotter, did he wake you up as well?' she demanded of Rhiannon. 'Just because he rises with the lark he expects everyone else to do the same. We girls need our beauty sleep, Pasqual, hasn't anyone ever told you?'

It sounded as though she knew every intimate detail about him, and Rhiannon went cold inside. Thank goodness they were going home today; she could not stand much more of this.

The drive across the island was over some of the most difficult terrain they had so far covered, the road pinned tenaciously to the mountainside, and Rhiannon clung to the edge of her seat. One error of judgement on Pasqual's part and they would plunge to their deaths.

They stopped frequently, and Rhiannon bought a red Chipude pot, hand-made by a village woman to exactly the same shape as the Guanche pots in the museum in Tenerife. In an obscure way it would remind her of Pasqual, she thought.

Ana purchased a blanket, woven and spun out of pure wool from the hardy mountain sheep, and she jeered at Pasqual because he refused to buy anything.

'What would I do with a pot or a blanket or even a rug?' he demanded.

'You could settle down and buy a house—then you'd have somewhere to put them,' said Ana archly.

'And get married, you mean?'

She nodded. 'You're not getting any younger.'

Rhiannon turned away, feeling distinctly embarrassed. Ana was virtually proposing. Didn't she know that his type never got married? She didn't look naïve, but she was certainly acting it.

It was a relief when they got back to the boat. Her engines were running when a boy came along the harbour waving an envelope. 'Señorita Howarth? Señorita Howarth?'

Pasqual frowned and stopped him, taking the paper and passing it to Rhiannon.

She was as mystified as he. Who could possibly be sending her a letter? Conscious of Ana and Pasqual watching, she tore it open and scanned the single sheet of paper. It was from Señor Calvos, the manager of the hotel. He hoped to catch her before she left. One of their receptionists had just handed in her notice. It was not the sort of work she was looking for, but it could and probably would lead to something else. It would mean her starting more or less straight away. Was she interested?

'What is it?' asked Pasqual, observing her silence.

'Nothing!' she said, her heart thudding, and to the boy who stood waiting, 'Just a moment.'

Going below, she scribbled her acceptance on the back of the letter and pushing it into the original envelope rushed back up to hand it to the boy.

But Pasqual beat him to it, taking the envelope out of her hand and reading its contents. His face was impasssive. Then he turned to the child. 'Tell Señor Calvos that the answer is no. The *Señorita* has changed her mind and does not require a job.' He delved into his pocket and dropped a handful of coins into the boy's hand, who smiled delightedly and ran away.

Ana gasped and Rhiannon exclaimed heatedly, 'How dare you! How dare you dictate what I do! It's my life, and if I want to work here then you won't stop me.'

'As a receptionist? Do you want to leave Cerrillo that badly?' A frown carved his brow.

'I wouldn't have accepted otherwise,' she said, chin high, eyes bright.

'I thought you loved the island?'

'I do. But things have changed.'

His lips tightened and he looked at her long and hard. 'I'm sorry, but I promised your father I'd keep an eye on you and I'd be failing in my duty if I let you take this job. You must come back to Cerrillo. We need you there.'

'I can't work with you,' she choked, 'and you can't make me stay at Cerrillo, you nor my father. I'll go wherever I want. This job is the chance I've been looking for—and I shan't be a receptionist forever. As soon as there's a vacancy in management, I shall be promoted. Señor Calvos was very impressed by my qualifications.'

'I bet he was!' sneered Pasqual. 'I happen to know Felipe Calvos, and the qualifications he's interested in are not the same ones you're talking about.'

Rhiannon tossed her head. 'You're lying! There was nothing improper in his attitude. He was a perfect gentleman—unlike you the first time we met.'

She did not really mean that, but he made her so mad she couldn't help herself.

'So now we know were we stand.' His tone was caustic, his eyes hard, his whole stance rejecting her. 'But that still doesn't mean I'll allow you to take this job. If it will make you happy I'll keep away from Cerrillo, but you're not going to work here, make no mistake about that.'

'Aren't I?' If he had spoken to her differently Rhiannon might have been persuaded. He had made her realise that far too often she got her own way. But she certainly wasn't going to let him get away with this. 'Who do you think you are? You can't dictate to me, no matter what my father says. I happen to think I'll be happy on Gomera.'

She tried to ignore the fact that she found Señor Calvos' offer insulting. But if it was the only job, and he had seen how desperate she was, he might have thought she would prefer that to nothing at all. She had not told him why she wanted to leave Cerrillo, but she had stressed her urgency to get away.

'No, Rhiannon. You'd be screaming for help within a week. Believe me, I know that character. Ana, untie the ropes. Let's get out of here.'

Rhiannon automatically turned to look at Ana. The girl had been listening and watching and was visibly upset, her face pale, her eyes disturbed, and she seemed not to realise that Pasqual was speaking to her.

'Ana!' he bellowed, and she jumped. 'Cast off, Ana, we're going.'

'I don't think you ought to speak to Rhiannon like that,' the girl said faintly.

'And what business is it of yours?' he barked.

She lifted her thin shoulders. 'None, I suppose, but I don't think she deserves being shouted at.'

'Rhiannon is a fool. She doesn't know what's good for her.' Muscles jerked in his jaw and his lips were so thin as to be almost invisible. But his voice softened. 'Are you going to untie those ropes or do I have to do it myself?'

'I'll do it,' Ana said weakly.

Minutes later they were out of the harbour and beginning their voyage home. Rhiannon went to her cabin, sitting cross-legged on the bed, fighting her inner torment. Was running away the answer? Could she, as Pasqual had suggested, be heading for more trouble?

To be truthful she didn't want to leave Cerrillo. So if she stayed and he kept away wouldn't that make life bearable again? She knew in her heart of hearts that it wouldn't. Pasqual had ruined her happiness. In fact it didn't matter to which part of the world she went he would be in her thoughts constantly. But on Cerrillo it would be worse, because that was where she had met him, where she would imagine him always. She must get away, she simply must.

When they got home she would ring Señor Calvos and explain there had been a mistake. By the time Pasqual found out she would be gone and he could do nothing about it.

'Rhiannon?' Ana tapped on her door and pushed it hesitantly open. 'Rhiannon, are you all right?' The girl looked worried and had still not regained the colour in her cheeks.

'I'm fine,' smiled Rhiannon, unable to think why this girl should be concerned.

Ana sat down on the edge of the bed. 'I don't like Pasqual to shout, he frightens me.' She looked a little girl all of a sudden. Gone was the provocative sexy image.

'You've been frightened like this before?' asked Rhiannon intuitively. 'A boy-friend? Your family?'

'My father,' admitted the girl. 'Before my parents were divorced. He used to get very violent.'

'But all men aren't the same. I'm sure Pasqual would never physically hurt anyone, least of all you. He loves you.'

Ana nodded her agreement.

'And he always treats you so gently and kindly.'

'I'm not afraid for myself, but for you. I've never seen him so violently angry.'

'Don't worry about me, I can take care of myself,' said Rhiannon strongly. Surprisingly she liked Ana and didn't want to hurt her further by declaring that she was in love with Pasqual too. It was a pointless love and best forgotten.

'If it's any consolation,' said Ana, 'I think he values your opinion. He won't make any drastic changes at the hotel, unless you approve. He praises you, he thinks you're quite remarkable.'

'Should I be flattered?' she asked drily.

'I think you should,' said Ana seriously. 'He's different with you from any other girl I've seen him with. I think you ought, perhaps, to revise your opinion of him.'

'It would be very difficult,' said Rhiannon. Ana didn't know about their affair; she thought their relationship a purely business one.

'You're not giving him a chance,' declared Ana. Some of the colour had returned to her cheeks and she stood up.

Rhiannon found it odd that this girl was trying to push them together. How trusting she was! Was she so confident of her own attraction, her power over Pasqual, that she felt he would never defect? Did she see her, Rhiannon, as a sexless nobody in the marriage stakes? Or was she genuinely so naïve that she never suspected he would make love to another girl?

'I think, Ana, if you don't mind I'd like some time on my own. I have a lot of thinking to do.'

'Of course,' said the dark girl at once, 'but I'm always prepared to listen. I want to help you, I really do.'

Rhiannon nodded and smiled. 'Thank you. I appreciate that.'

How long she remained sitting there Rhiannon did not know. Perhaps it was hours, perhaps minutes, but she was no nearer reaching a solution when Ana called out to say that lunch was ready.

Although the thought of food sickened her Rhiannon knew she dared not stay in her cabin any longer. She had no wish for Pasqual to come in search of her. She wanted no further private conversations with him.

But Pasqual did not join them for lunch, declaring, according to Ana, that it was unsafe to leave the ship on automatic rudder and besides he was not hungry.

Was he still angry with her? wondered Rhiannon. Not that she cared. If he never spoke to her again he would be doing her a favour.

At length, when it was dark, they arrived back at Cerrillo. It had been a tormented journey, Ana bravely attempting to make conversation but giving up when neither of them responded.

Never had the hotel been more welcome. Rhiannon went straight to her private quarters and left Pasqual to look after Ana. He would make sure the girl was comfortable.

She showered and made herself a cup of hot chocolate and sat on the balcony sipping it, forgetting time, forgetting everything except her doomed love for Pasqual, and the pain of him inviting another girl to share their last days. Anyone else would have been welcome, to relieve the tension, but not one of his girl-friends. It was the final humiliation.

The stars filled the heavens with myriad sparkling lights, the moon silvered a path across the sea, and cicadas chirred. But so far as Rhiannon was concerned the island had lost its magic—and all because of Pasqual.

Eventually she retired to bed, but sleep eluded her. She could not help thinking about Ana and Pasqual. It hurt, the thought of them together. How long would it go on? How long did he plan to keep her here?

When morning came she felt she hadn't slept at all, and the first thing she did was put through a call to Señor Calvos.

'There's been a misunderstanding,' she said. 'I do want that job. My—er—friend, who gave the errand boy the answer, didn't know. I didn't say I'd approached you in case nothing came of it.'

'I see,' he said slowly and thoughtfully. 'Would your friend be Pasqual Giminez, by any chance?'

Rhiannon frowned, feeling suddenly uneasy. 'He is. Does that make any difference?'

She could almost see him smile. 'Not in the least. In fact it would give me the greatest of pleasure to get one over on him. We are old acquaintances and never see eye to eye. When can you start?'

Relief flooded over her. They were enemies, that was all. Pasqual had made up that tale about him lusting after women just to frighten her. 'There are things I need to sort out, and getting there by ferry will take a while. In a week I should think.' And with a bit of luck Pasqual would have gone.

'Not good enough,' he said briskly. 'I have a friend who will come and fetch you—say, the day after tomorrow. Can you manage that?'

'Yes, I think so.' Rhiannon wondered why she suddenly did not feel so happy about the situation. She was getting away from Pasqual, wasn't she? What more did she want?

Miguel was pleased to see her back, but he had coped admirably in her absence and enjoyed the feeling of power. After his first reservations about the place he now raved over it. Rhiannon felt reasonably happy about leaving things in his hands. Not that she ought to worry, she told herself. The hotel wasn't her responsibility any longer.

Checking through the register she noticed that Pasqual and Ana were booked into rooms next to each other. How very convenient, she thought drily, swallowing a painful lump in her throat.

She spent the day making sure everything was in order and saw neither of them. Miguel said they had gone off together that morning. 'I expect he is going to show her the island,' he added. 'She is a very pretty girl, is she not? And I am glad that he has found himself a nice girl-friend, because that leaves you for me. He was not pleased, that we went out together. I thought that perhaps you and he were——' He looked at her expectantly.

'No,' said Rhiannon at once. 'Pasqual's never felt that way about me. But I don't think he agrees with staff fraternising.'

'Does that mean you won't come out with me again?' he asked despondently.

She shook her head and smiled. 'Somehow I don't think we're going to have much time for pleasure.' She did not tell him she was planning to leave. She would tell no one, not until the last minute. It was cowardly, she knew, but she did not want anything to go wrong.

Pasqual and Ana had not come back when she went to bed. She tried to tell herself she didn't care, that if he wanted to spend the whole day with this other girl then it was all right with her. But deep down it hurt, and no amount of reasoning with herself made any difference.

The next day she spent most of her time packing and writing letters. Her father wouldn't be pleased when he heard what she had done, but there was nothing he could do about it.

When she checked that everything was running smoothly Miguel told her that yet again Pasqual and Ana had gone out for the day. Rhiannon mentally crossed her fingers that they would go off tomorrow too, then she wouldn't need to worry about him seeing her leave.

But the next morning everything went wrong. To begin with, after tossing and turning for most of the night, she overslept and when she finally went through to the hotel to make last-minute checks and tell Miguel that she was leaving Pasqual himself was in the office.

It was impossible to quell the flood of feeling that surged through her. She had not realised how much she had missed him these last two days. And soon he would be out of her life for ever!

'Where's Ana?' she asked, not realising how bitter her voice sounded.

'Still in bed, I imagine,' he replied. 'We've had a hectic couple of days. Ana has fallen in love with your island. I never expected it. She's a fun-loving girl who likes a good time, but she actually said that she couldn't understand why you wanted to leave.'

Rhiannon's senses alerted. Did he know? Had he found out that she was going today? Or was she being over-sensitive. 'Does that mean she's going to settle down here herself?' With you, she added silently.

'Anything's possible with Ana. One never knows which way her fancy's going to turn. I'd like to see Miguel. Would you mind finding him for me? He's in the restaurant, I believe.'

It was obvious he had no wish to hold her in conversation, and Rhiannon's lips were set as she left the room. His actions convinced her that she was doing the right thing.

She found Miguel, and after passing on Pasqual's message told him that she would be leaving today and not coming back. 'Here is a note for Señor Giminez, but please don't give it to him until after I've gone. I don't want him trying to stop me.'

Miguel frowned. 'What is this? I do not understand?'

'I can't remain here,' she explained. 'It's not the same now the hotel's no longer my father's, but Pasqual refuses to understand how I feel and I know he'll try to persuade me to stay. Once I've gone it will be too late.'

He looked sad. 'I will miss you, Rhiannon.'

'You won't have time to miss me,' she smiled. 'I'm actually doing you a favour. Pasqual will probably make you manager now, you did very well while we were away.'

'Really?' He beamed his pleasure and almost did a dance on the spot.

'Now, don't forget, tell him nothing until I've gone. I'm being picked up at two so if you wait until dinner, unless he misses me before then, I will be safe.'

But it was going to be tricky getting away without Pasqual seeing her. She wished with all her heart that he had taken Ana out again. Maybe—when the girl got up? But that was wishful thinking. She could not rely on it.

She stood her cases by the door. The furniture was covered with dust sheets, the fridge cleaned out, all perishable goods disposed of. When the hotel was sold it was agreed that she could use these quarters for as long as she needed, but she could not imagine Pasqual keeping them available for her in case she ever came back. By leaving she was forgoing all rights, and it would be up to her father and Pasqual what happened to the furniture.

When she ventured outside with her cases at a quarter to the hour there was no one in sight, and she could not believe her good fortune when she made it all the way down to the harbour without bumping into anyone.

She was hot and perspiring by the time she got there, the cases having grown heavier with each step. The only strange ship in the harbour was one moored next to Pasqual's and she looked for the friend of Señor Calvos.

But all seemed deserted. She stepped on board and peered inside. 'Is anyone there?'

'Right here,' came Pasqual's familiar voice from behind her.

CHAPTER TEN

RHIANNON whirled in surprise at the sound of Pasqual's voice, her heart plummeting, her eyes wide. He was the last person she wanted to see.

His smile looked threatening. 'How fortunate it was I arrived when I did, otherwise you would have left without my knowing it.'

'Which is what I intended doing,' she snapped. 'Where's the man who's supposed to meet me?'

'Enjoying a drink on my boat,' he replied smoothly. 'Why don't you join us?'

'No, thanks,' she choked. 'I'll wait here.'

Savage anger tautened his face. 'Rhiannon, do you realise what a serious mistake you are making? Running away is no answer to a problem at the best of times, but running into the arms of Felipe Calvos is foolhardy. Was my warning in vain?'

She lifted her chin defiantly. 'Why should I take any notice of you? You've never done me any favours.'

His lips tightened. 'You'll have no one to turn to if things go wrong.'

'I have no one anyway,' she cried. 'I've got used to looking after myself.'

'Is there nothing I can say that will make you change your mind?' His hands were on her arms suddenly, his voice more gentle, his eyes searching her face. 'I know how much it means to you here. I meant it when I said that I would leave Cerrillo. Is that the answer?'

'Don't flatter yourself,' she snapped. 'You can stay or go, it makes no difference. You've already done the damage.'

It crucified her to deny herself of him. Despite the way he had treated her, despite everything, she still loved him. But it was a pointless love, and this was the only way she would get him out of her system.

His grip on her arms tightened. 'Is that your last word?'

Rhiannon compressed her lips and nodded, even managing to look him in the eye, but she was glad he could not see her heart breaking.

A sigh shuddered through him and he turned away, his eyes hooded. 'In that case I will detain you no longer.'

He disappeared and from the depths of his ship appeared a tough-looking muscular man, his arms deeply tattooed. Rhiannon did not like the look of him and almost changed her mind, but his manner belied his looks. 'Señorita Howarth? Welcome on board. My name is Juan, and it is my privilege to escort you safely to Gomera.' He stowed her cases below and started the engine. Of Pasqual there was no sign as he steered the ship carefully out of the harbour.

Rhiannon felt like breaking down and crying. Was this the end? Was this the last she would see of the man she loved? Why did she feel like crying when it was her own decision? She wasn't being forced to leave—except by fate.

The voyage seemed never-ending. She sat down, she stood at the rail. She walked the decks and she went below. Juan watched her but said nothing, his big face impassive.

It was late evening when they finally arrived at Gomera. She had not eaten all day, nor did she want to, and when Señor Calvos had a table set for the two

of them in a private corner of the dining room she could
have spat in his eye.

Instead she smiled sweetly. 'Thank you very much,
but I'm not hungry. I am tired, though. Do you think
I could go straight to my room?'

Why hadn't she noticed before that his eyes were all
over her? Why had she ignored what Pasqual said? But
she was used to dealing with men like this creepy
Spaniard. She would soon put him in his place.

Rhiannon did not expect to sleep. It had been an
excuse that she was tired. But after unpacking and
stowing her clothes in the clean but tiny room, she lay
on the bed and knew no more until her alarm sounded.

Life settled into a routine of work and sleep, of
fighting off Felipe's lecherous advances and trying to
forget about Pasqual.

She discovered that the last receptionist had left
because of Felipe, one in a long line who had resented
his groping hands. And she had walked straight into
it—despite being warned—with no place she could run.
Except, perhaps, to her father.

But she was loath to do this. It was a last resort. She
had metaphorically made her bed, so she must lie in it.
Perhaps Felipe would eventually take the hint and
leave her alone?

Week followed week, and if it hadn't been for Felipe
she would have enjoyed the job. It made a change to
have no responsibilities, to pass enquiries she could not
deal with on to the management. She had more time
to herself than ever before and often went exploring
with one of the waitresses—an English girl about her
own age.

But Pasqual was never out of her mind for long. Was
Ana still on Cerrillo? she wondered. How was their
romance progressing? Would it be as hard for Ana

when the end inevitably came? Was the girl destined to heartbreak?

And still Felipe continued to harass her. The more she rejected him the more determined he became. One night, when she was on late duty and the hotel was particularly quiet, he called her into the office.

The moment he closed the door behind her she knew it spelled trouble. The door was always kept open if they left the desk, that way they could see if anyone needed attention.

'Felipe,' she said, 'I can't leave the desk unmanned.'

'We will hear if anyone comes,' he said calmly, the smile she was learning to dread curving his lips. It meant he was in the mood for love—and this time it looked as though he meant business.

'I'd rather the door was left open,' she persisted, going towards it, her hand outstretched. But in this she made a mistake. He took her hand and pulled her hard against him. 'Why do you keep fighting me?' His breath was hot in her ear and smelled of rum. 'I know you like me, that's why you took this job. Don't play hard to get any more. You're driving me crazy!'

His hands were all over her, feeling every curve, and it was impossible to ignore his arousal. 'I do not like you, Felipe,' she snapped, trying to avoid his offending mouth. 'Let me go, will you? Let me go!'

She struggled and kicked, but no avail, it seemed to excite him further, and when his mouth finally fixed itself on hers she felt physically ill. Clearly fighting was getting her nowhere, so instead she went limp in his arms, standing quite still, sagging like a rag doll.

This did not please him at all. 'Rhiannon, respond to me,' he grated, his eyes brilliant, his face flushed. 'Kiss me. Kiss me!'

'If I kiss you,' she said slowly and deliberately, 'I shall be sick.'

He could not believe he had heard her correctly and relaxed his grip for a moment, his eyes widening, his face suddenly pale.

Rhiannon dived for the door and wrenched it open just as his hand fell heavily on her shoulder. 'You little bitch!' he choked. 'How dare you insult me like that! Come here. I'll show you whether——'

He stopped when he realised that someone was standing at the desk, and Rhiannon, her hair awry, her face flushed, looked across—and saw her father.

'Daddy!' Tears that she had stemmed for so long flooded to the surface, racing down her cheeks, blurring her vision. She lifted the flap on the desk and walked into his arms. 'Oh, Daddy, please take me home!'

They talked well into the night, sitting in her room, his arm comfortingly about her. 'You had no right,' she grumbled, 'conspiring with Pasqual. The whole holiday was a disaster!'

'So I've heard.' His face was rueful. 'I'm sorry, I really did think that you two were made for each other.'

Rhiannon grimaced. 'How I wish that were true! I love Pasqual. I went through a whole period when I hated him, but now I know I really do love him. Do you know Ana?'

He nodded.

'She's another one of his loves. He was actually seeing her at the same time as me. I doubt it will last. I'm best rid of him.'

She fell asleep in his arms and the next morning awoke to find herself tucked in bed still fully dressed and her father asleep in the chair.

Smiling tenderly, she touched his face. 'Daddy, wake up!' She felt much better and a little ashamed of her outburst. She who always claimed to be in complete control, an independent adult who could take care of herself.

'Where am I? Oh, yes, I remember. Rhiannon my love, how are you?'

'More importantly, how are you?' she smiled. 'I bet you're stiff. Why didn't you take the bed?'

'Because your need was greater. You'd had a pretty traumatic experience. What a lecher that man is! How long's it been going on? Why didn't you leave?'

She shook her head. 'I don't know. I was so intent on running away from Pasqual that I shut my eyes to everything else.'

'You could have come to me,' he said in a quiet hurt voice.

'I should have done,' she admitted. 'It's just that I wanted to stay in the Canaries. They're my home now. I love it here.'

'Me too,' he admitted ruefully. 'I've come back, Rhiannon. There was nothing for me in England. Frank died, a couple of weeks ago and——'

'Oh, I'm sorry,' she said at once.

'And you're all I have left. I thought I'd buy a house on Cerrillo, not too far from the hotel, so that I could see you every day.'

'Are you forgetting I don't work there any longer?' she asked gently.

'Pasqual's prepared to take you back.'

Her head shot up. 'That's big of him! Who's saying I want to?' But her heart fluttered at the thought of seeing him again.

'If I know you, Rhiannon, it's what you want most. It must have broken your heart to leave Yurena.'

She nodded. 'Will Pasqual be there?'

'No.'

This in itself was a relief, and she asked no further questions, not wanting to hear whether Ana was with him still. It was best she remained in ignorance.

'I think we ought to get washed and changed and be on our way.'

'A good idea,' she grinned. 'Who's going to use the bathroom first?'

It was uncomfortable saying goodbye to Felipe. She half expected him to insist on her working out her notice, and if her father hadn't been present she guessed he might have. But Tony Howarth was at his imperious best and they left with no argument and her wages in her hand.

It was a long slow journey on the ferry and they were both exhausted and sweaty when they arrived. Alterations had already started, and it was like a knife twisting in her heart to see the new extension going up. But at least nothing had changed in their private quarters, and when a meal was sent through to them from the hotel kitchen it was just like old times. They went to bed tired but happy, and Rhiannon slept in until ten the following morning.

During the next few days she helped her father with his house-hunting and was careful to make no mention of Pasqual. He, in his turn, did not bring him into the conversation. But he could see she was unhappy, that her mind was frequently on other things, and he guessed that it was the man she loved.

'You can't go on like this,' he said one evening when they were sipping their nightcap on the balcony. 'I'm not one to interfere, Rhiannon, I never have been. But have you looked at yourself in the mirror lately? You're half the girl you were. No man is worth worrying yourself to death over. You must see him and sort things out. Get it clear in your mind one way or the other.'

'It is clear,' she said sadly. 'He doesn't love me.'

'Then why are you still mooning over him? Find yourself another boy-friend, for goodness' sake. You

can't say you don't get the opportunity. We have all
sorts pass through here.'

'But none whom I fancy. Don't try and push me into
a relationship I don't want, Daddy.'

'So how long are you going to make me wait? I
would like some grandchildren, Rhiannon, while I'm
young enough to enjoy them.'

He was right, she was being foolish. And since
Miguel was still interested she began dating him. But
it didn't work. When he kissed her she thought of
Pasqual. And when he didn't kiss her she thought of
Pasqual. She couldn't seem to shake him out of her
mind.

There were times when, if she had known where he
was, she would have confronted him. He had once, a
lifetime ago, sworn to love her. Were there any of those
feelings left, or had it all been a pack of lies? Was there
any hope for the future, or must she push him out of
her mind for ever?

She said some of this to her father the next day.

He looked at her sadly and thoughtfully. 'I have a
confession to make, Rhiannon. I wasn't being entirely
truthful when I said I didn't know where Pasqual was.'

Rhiannon frowned.

'He asked me to keep his whereabouts secret.'

'Secret? Why would he want to do that?'

'He loves you, Rhiannon, very much, but he asked
me not to tell you where he is unless I'm sure you love
him too and can't live without him. Unhappily he was
certain this would never be the case. You made a very
good job of convincing him. I think now, though, that
the time has come.'

Rhiannon closed her eyes. 'I wish you hadn't told
me that, Daddy.' Even though her heart had begun to
sing. Pasqual loved her! Not Ana, not any of the other
girls, but her. A miracle had happened.

'You said a minute ago you wanted to see him?' frowned her father.

'But if I turn up on his doorstep he'll know why,' she protested. It will be too embarrassing. Why do I have to make the first move? Why can't he come to me?'

'Because he tried and failed,' said her father with a heavy sigh. 'If you don't go you'll commit yourself to a lifetime's unhappiness. You must know that? You have to make the most of life while you can. Who knows when our time will come? Grab your happiness with both hands, Rhiannon. Don't be afraid to tell the man you love him.' There was a break in her father's voice. 'Swallow your pride.'

He was thinking about the way her mother had been snatched from him, she knew, but for him to say that Pasqual had tried and failed was ludicrous. Pasqual hadn't tried very hard at all. He had convinced her when he invited Ana to join them that he was a man who never remained true to one woman for long.

What sort of a line had he spun her father? she wondered. But if she didn't go to see him he would be in her mind always. This was the only way to sort things out and lay his ghost for ever. 'Give me his address,' she said quietly. It would take courage, but she would do it.

He opened a drawer in his bureau and handed her a slip of paper. As she glanced briefly at the address, with the intention of slipping it into her pocket, the name Gran Canaria leapt out at her.

Ana lived on Gran Canaria! Rhiannon had heard her mention something to Pasqual about it. Excitement, which had begun to leap along her nerve streams, changed to despair.

'Whose is this address?' she asked her father. 'Is it Ana's?'

He looked at her sagely. 'Does it make any difference?'

'I'll say it does!' she cried, her eyes pained. 'If he's living with her then no way am I going. There'd be no point.'

'It's his father's house,' he said with a quiet smile. 'And I understand he's away at the moment.'

Somewhat mollified, Rhiannon pushed the paper into her pocket. 'I'll give it some thought.'

It took her two days to make up her mind and a lot of firm talking to herself before she finally left for Gran Canaria. When she found the address in Las Palmas her heart beat so painfully that she wondered whether it was worth the agony she was putting herself through.

The house itself was a striking example of nineteenth-century Canarian architecture, with arches and pillars and balconies all finely detailed, and a verandah running right round the building affording shade at any time of day.

Rhiannon walked straight up to the main entrance without appreciating its beauty and rang the bell. She did not expect Pasqual himself to answer the door. He might not even be at home. In fact she hoped he wasn't. But neither did she expect Ana to open it. Had her father been lying? Or had he simply omitted to mention that they were living together?

Her first instinct when she saw the dark girl was to turn and run. But before she could do any more than change her expression Ana rushed forward and hugged her. 'Rhiannon! How pleased I am to see you. Do come in.' And there was no escape.

'I was so shocked when you left. I couldn't believe it. I've thought about you often. How are you getting on?' She led her into a large room at the back of the house.

Rhiannon pulled a face. 'I'm not. I'm back at Yurena—with my father. He's looking for a house.'

There was something puzzling about Ana's attitude. If the girl was in love with Pasqual surely she would have been relieved when she, Rhiannon, left the island? And she certainly wouldn't be pleased to see her now. What did it mean?

'That's nice,' said Ana. 'To tell you the truth I couldn't understand him, nor you, leaving Cerrillo. It's beautiful. I wouldn't mind living there myself—if there was a bit more life,' she added with a laugh. 'Perhaps I'll settle there when I'm older. Pasqual's in his study. I'll tell him you're here.' And before Rhiannon could stop her the girl had fled the room.

Rhiannon looked at the tapestries on the walls, the carved figurines, the portraits. It was like a museum. It had an unlived-in feeling—and yet it was beautiful. She moved to the window and looked out at the well-tended lawns, the palms and roses, hibiscus and frangipani, and a splendid specimen of a dragon tree with its thick bulbous branches and canopy of spiky leaves.

Have I done the right thing in coming here? she asked herself, and was wondering whether to quietly leave when a sound behind made her turn.

She almost couldn't recognise Pasqual. His cheeks were hollow, his eyes sunken, and there was a curious haunted air about him. He looked at her as though she were a stranger.

'Pasqual, are you ill?' Rhiannon took an involuntary step forward, but stopped when she saw the coldness in his eyes.

'What are you doing here?' he asked bluntly, almost rudely, giving her no encouragement, no indication that his feelings were anything other than hostile.

'I—I wanted to see you.'

'Who told you where to find me?'

'My father.' Now he would know. It would be easier. He would help her to find the right words.

'Are you still working in Gomera?'

She shook her head.

His eyes narrowed. 'That didn't last long. What happened?'

Deciding that honesty was the best policy, Rhiannon said, 'You were right about Felipe Calvos. He made a nuisance of himself. I couldn't stay.'

His eyes froze. 'He didn't force himself——'

'No,' she cut in firmly, 'but if I'd stayed any longer goodness knows what might have happened.' A shudder raced through her as she thought of that last incident, and not for the first time she thanked her lucky stars that her father had turned up when he did.

'I'd have killed him,' he said beneath his breath, but Rhiannon heard and felt a flicker of hope.

'I'm living with my father now at the hotel—I hope you don't mind? As soon as he finds a house I shall naturally move in with him.'

'You were happy, I take it, that he had returned?'

She nodded.

'And now you're out of work. Is it your old job back that you're after? Is that why you're here?'

Only the fact that he looked tired and ill stopped Rhiannon from making a heated retort. 'No. I wanted to see you again, to find out how things were going with you—and Ana.' The girl's name slipped out and she bit her bottom lip. 'I'm sorry, I shouldn't have said that. It's no business of mine.'

He shrugged. 'Ana, as you saw, is in the best of health and spirits. Whereas I am suffering from——' He smiled wearily. 'You tell me what I'm suffering from?'

Rhiannon frowned, feeling puzzled. 'How am I to know?'

A muscle jerked in his jaw. 'Why did your father give
ou my address?'

Warily she said, 'Because he thought I ought to
know.'

'Why?'

She looked down at her hands. Why was he making
her go through all this? He must know, if what her
father had said was true. 'Because—because I needed
o see you—and now I wish I hadn't. I've got my
answer.'

'Have you, Rhiannon? Have you? Things are not
always what they seem. You're wondering what's
wrong with me? Why Ana is here? What my relationship with her is?'

Miserably she nodded.

'I will tell you—after you've told me why you came
here today.'

Rhiannon closed her eyes and took a deep breath,
fighting a choking lump in her throat. It was now or
never. Still with her eyes closed she said, 'Because—I
love you, Pasqual.' She felt the blood rush up under
her skinff6andvas scared to look at him. It was not an
easy admission when she remained in ignorance of his
feelings. Had he told her that he loved her she would
have declared her love proudly. As it was, she felt like
creeping under a stone and dying. Why didn't he speak,
say something, anything? Even that he loved Ana?
Anything was better than this silence. Reluctantly she
lifted her lids and looked at him, catching her breath
when she saw the hope in his eyes.

'Say that again, Rhiannon.'

Hope! Not amusement, or ridicule, or rejection. But
hope. He wanted her to repeat that she loved him, as
though he could not quite believe what he had heard.
It did not necessarily mean that he returned her love,
but all the same he was not making fun of her.

'It's true, Pasqual. I love you. I always have. I was mixed up for a time, but not any longer.' And now it was up to him. If he loved and wanted her she was here. If it was Ana he loved then all he had to do was tell her to go, and that would be an end to her uncertainty. She could start a new life knowing that he had no part in it.

It was Pasqual's turn to close his eyes. He lifted his chin and clasped his hands as though he were praying and when he looked at her there was a new light in his eyes. 'I never thought I'd hear you say that again, Rhiannon. Have you any idea at all of the suffering you've put me through?'

'Not until this moment,' she said softly. 'Does it mean that——'

'I love you,' he said, his voice strong now and loud. 'Rhiannon, I love you. I've felt I was dying these last few weeks. I couldn't eat, I couldn't work, I couldn't do anything except think about you.'

Everything inside Rhiannon curled up into tight knots. She had done this to him. By rejecting him, by telling him time and time again that she did not love him, she had sentenced him to a living death. Would he ever be able to forgive her?

'What can I say?' she whispered achingly. 'I never knew. I truly never knew.'

'You were too busy thinking the worst of me.'

'Most men I'd met were after only one thing.'

He smiled. 'So was I. You. All of you. For my wife. Come here, Rhiannon. Let me see if you feel as good in my arms as I remember.'

Every pulse in her body made itself felt as she walked slowly towards him, the blood pounded in her head and her heart raced unevenly. She stopped within a hair's breadth of him and they stood looking deeply into each other's eyes before with a groan he pulled her against him.

His heart was as unbalanced as her own, his skin dewed with perspiration, and he held her so tightly she thought her bones would snap.

When she looked at him there were tears in his eyes, rolling slowly down his cheeks. Without a word she wiped them away and pressed her lips to the dampness of his jaw.

'I can't believe this is happening,' he muttered thickly. 'Tell me you're real, Rhiannon. Tell me it's not a dream. I've had so many of them I feel sure this must be another.'

'It's no dream,' she said softly, moving her lips to his mouth, needing him now desperately.

'No!' he groaned. 'Once we start that I shan't be able to stop, and there's so much I have to tell you. I've not been fair to you, Rhiannon. I've hurt you. I have to put things right.'

'Ana?' she ventured timidly. But what did she care about Ana now? He loved her, he had said as much. This girl meant nothing to him. She could afford to be generous.

'Yes, Ana. Sit down, Rhiannon. No, not there,' when she would have joined him on the couch. 'Over there, where I can look at you.'

She smiled, agreeing it would be hard to talk if they sat together. Their bodies hungered for each other and once the floodgates opened there would be no stopping them.

'Rhiannon, I've loved you from the first moment I set eyes on you. I came to look over your hotel and fell irrevocably in love. The fact that I wanted Yurena had nothing at all to do with you. You do believe that?'

She nodded.

'You've no idea of the shock I felt when I came back and found you a different person. I'd been going around like a cat with two tails. I'd never loved a woman as much as I loved you. There have been others, admittedly, but you were the only one I ever wanted for a wife—and suddenly you'd gone cold on me. I couldn't believe it. I felt as though you'd dealt me a death sentence.'

'I'm sorry,' she whispered, her eyes hungrily devouring every inch of him. She had given him those gaunt features, made him ill when he should have been bursting with love. 'I'm truly sorry.'

He shook his head. 'It can only have done good. If your love hadn't been strong enough you wouldn't be here now.'

'And yours?' she whispered.

'I would have loved you to the end of my days—but I'd done all I could.'

'Like kidnapping me?'

Pasqual smiled ruefully. 'I thought if I got you on your own I'd be able to make you love me again. I knew you were strong-willed, but never realised exactly how much. It was like battering my head against a brick wall.'

'I've learned the error of my ways,' she admitted quietly. 'I shall never think of just myself again. But did you have to seek solace with Ana? Have you any idea of the torment you put me through?'

'It was intentional,' he said. 'It was a calculated risk. I'd tried everything else. I knew you were jealous of her. That knowledge was the only thing that kept me sane. My hopes were lifted at one stage—when I spent the night in your bed. I'm only human, Rhiannon, I'm afraid I couldn't keep my hands off you. Then I realised you were dreaming and your response meant nothing at all.'

Rhiannon gasped. 'Oh, Pasqual, I thought it was a dream too. I wasn't sure. I was so embarrassed I was afraid to face you the next morning. You'll never know how relieved I was that you'd left the ship.' Then her mouth tightened. 'Had you gone to see Ana?'

He grinned and nodded. 'I love Ana, but not in the way you think. Ana—is—my sister.'

Rhiannon gasped. 'Oh! You—you—monster!' And then burst into laughter. 'You made her pose as your girl-friend?'

He nodded. 'Ana was to wait at the hotel in Gomera and discreetly observe us before making her presence known. If things looked good then she was my sister, if we were none too friendly, then she was to act the part of a very possessive girl-friend. I knew it wouldn't be difficult because since our parents' divorce we've been very close. But my plot didn't work,' he continued sadly. 'It only made things worse. I gave your father my address, and all that was left for me to do was hope that time would be my saviour.'

'Daddy's a wise old man,' she smiled. 'He knew how you felt, how I felt, but he made me work things out for myself. All I needed was a little push at the end— and how glad I am that I came. Oh, Pasqual, I can't bear to see you like this! It's all my fault. How can you still love me?' She got up and ran over to him, her love shining in her eyes.

'How can I not?' His arms welcomed her as she sat on his lap and their mouths finally met in a kiss that drugged their senses, made them oblivious to time, to surroundings, to life itself.

They had lost each other for so long, and now they were afraid to let go. They drank hungrily of the love that was their life stream, their bodies pressed achingly close, their hearts pounding in unison.

It was a long time before they came back to earth, Rhiannon's eyes shining as they gazed lovingly into Pasqual's.

'I'm never going to let you out of my sight again,' he said, his fingertips tracing the outline of her lips. 'You're mine now, Rhiannon, mine for ever. There's just one thing worrying me—Miguel.'

'He never meant anything to me,' she said at once. 'He was a balm to my wounded ego, that's all.'

'He didn't—make love to you?'

'Heavens, no!' she cried. 'Our relationship wasn't like that.'

He looked relieved. 'I'm going to marry you as soon as it's humanly possible, Rhiannon. I'm taking no chances that you'll change your mind about me again.'

'I won't.' She shook her head strongly. 'I won't, I promise you. Shall we tell Ana? She must be dying to know what's going on.'

He smiled, and they stood up and went and found Ana in the kitchen. 'You don't have to tell me,' she laughed. 'I came in once but you were—er—otherwise engaged. I'm so happy for you. I've never had a sister, Rhiannon, but if I could choose then it would be you. I'm sorry I had to deceive you. I hated doing it.'

There were hugs and kisses and much laughter and then Pasqual said, 'I think we ought to ring your father, Rhiannon. I bet he's beside himself with anxiety.'

'Not anxiety,' she laughed. 'He'll know what's going on. But let's tell him all the same. I'm so glad he came back. Without him I don't think we'd ever have got together. I hope he finds a nice house—and I don't want to live too far away from him.' A sudden frown shadowed her smile. 'Where will we live, Pasqual?'

'I know you like Cerrillo,' he said, 'but it's not really the ideal spot to bring up a young family. How about—here?'

'In this beautiful house? But—your father? It belongs to him, doesn't it?'

'Not any longer. He's gone to America. I think this place is large enough to accommodate all of us without anyone losing their privacy. And the grounds are extensive enough for you and your father not to feel that you're part of the commercialised city that you both hate. You'll have the best of both worlds. What do you say?'

'I think it's a wonderful idea,' she smiled. If he had asked her to go to the icy wastes of Siberia she would have gone.

'How about me?' asked Ana, trying her hardest to look hurt.

'I imagine we can put up with you—until you find yourself a husband,' Pasqual smiled.

'Which could be quite a long time,' she said. 'You've spoilt me, Pasqual. My husband will have to measure up to you—and that's saying something! There are not many men like you about.'

Rhiannon agreed wholeheartedly. Pasqual was unique—which was why she loved him. She did not deserve him, she had treated him scandalously, and it would take the rest of her life to make up. But it would be a labour of love, and she gazed at him reverently. 'I do love you, Pasqual.'

He held her close. 'I think we ought to go up to my room and you can begin to show me exactly how much.'

Ana laughed, not in the least embarrassed. 'Don't you think you ought to make that call first? You have so much loving to catch up on it could be several days before anyone sees you again.'

'That doesn't sound a bad idea,' said Pasqual.

And Rhiannon nodded her head in agreement.

Harlequin Presents

Coming Next Month

1047 RECKLESS Amanda Carpenter
A routine assignment to South America turns into a nightmare when Leslie's flight is hijacked. She draws on all her strength to save fellow journalist Scott Bennett, only to discover the real test is of her ability to love again.

1048 STRIKE AT THE HEART Emma Darcy
Sunny King is everything Jackie Mulholland disapproves of: rich, reckless and overwhelmingly arrogant. So she's disturbed by the attraction he seems to hold for her two young sons. She's even more disturbed by her own attraction to him.

1049 CARLISLE PRIDE Leigh Michaels
Brooke has more than her share of pride. It was pride that made her break her engagement to Ty Marshall after finding him in her stepmother's arms; and it's pride that now makes her refuse to sell Oakley Manor...but refusing Ty again will cost more than pride.

1050 TAGGART'S WOMAN Carole Mortimer
To inherit her rightful share of the family airline business, Heather is forced to marry her late father's partner, Daniel Taggart. For Heather the arrangement seems a little like hell—and heaven.

1051 TRUE ENCHANTER Susan Napier
Joanna's not impressed by the superficial glamour of the film world, which is why she's the perfect chaperone for her actress niece. But she's not what director Richard Marlow expects. She can see right through him, as he does her. Have they both met their match?

1052 OPEN TO INFLUENCE Frances Roding
A girl on her own, hopelessly in love with her married boss and without a job because of it, is hardly the ideal guardian for an orphaned three year old. So Rosemary is in no position to refuse Nicholas Powers, even if it means giving up a life—and love—of her own.

1053 BROKEN SILENCE Kate Walker
When Jill negotiates her wages as a temporary nanny to Luke Garrett's small son, she doesn't bargain for the claim her employer makes on her own heart. She should have.

1054 THIS MAN'S MAGIC Stephanie Wyatt
By asking her father for an introduction to Lucas Armory, Sorrel starts a chain of events that turns her life upside down. For Luke doesn't believe she's Felix Valentine's daughter, and worse, he accuses her of stealing his company's latest jewelry designs.

Available in January wherever paperback books are sold, or through Harlequin Reader Service:

In the U.S.
901 Fuhrmann Blvd.
P.O. Box 1397
Buffalo, N.Y. 14240-1397

In Canada
P.O. Box 603
Fort Erie, Ontario
L2A 5X3

An enticing
new historical romance!

Spring Will Come

SHERRY DeBORDE

It was 1852, and the steamy South was in its last hours of
gentility. Camille Braxton Beaufort went searching for the
one man she knew she could trust, and under his protec-
tion had her first lesson in love....

Available in October at your favorite retail outlet, or reserve your copy for September ship-
ping by sending your name, address, zip or postal code, along with a check or money order
for $4.70 (includes 75¢ postage and handling) payable to Worldwide Library to:

In the U.S.	In Canada
Worldwide Library	Worldwide Library
901 Fuhrmann Blvd.	P.O. Box 609
P.O. Box 1325	Fort Erie, Ontario
Buffalo, NY 14269-1325	L2A 5X3

Please specify book title with your order.

 **WORLDWIDE LIBRARY**

SPR-1

ATTRACTIVE, SPACE SAVING BOOK RACK

Display your most prized novels on this handsome and sturdy book rack. The hand-rubbed walnut finish will blend into your library decor with quiet elegance, providing a practical organizer for your favorite hard-or soft-covered books.

Only $9.95

Approximately 16" x 8" when assembled

Assembles in seconds!

To order, rush your name, address and zip code, along with a check or money order for $10.70* ($9.95 plus 75¢ postage and handling) payable to *Harlequin Reader Service*:

Harlequin Reader Service
Book Rack Offer
901 Fuhrmann Blvd.
P.O. Box 1396
Buffalo, NY 14269-1396

Offer not available in Canada.

*New York and Iowa residents add appropriate sales tax.

BKR-1A